AMBER BROWN
HORSES AROUND

Discover all the Amber Brown chapter books

Amber Brown Is Not a Crayon

You Can't Eat Your Chicken Pox, Amber Brown

Amber Brown Goes Fourth

Amber Brown Wants Extra Credit

Forever Amber Brown

Amber Brown Sees Red

Amber Brown Is Feeling Blue

I, Amber Brown

Amber Brown Is Green With Envy

Amber Brown Is Tickled Pink

Amber Brown Is on the Move

Paula Danziger's

AMBER BROWN
HORSES AROUND

Written by Bruce Coville
and Elizabeth Levy
illustrations by Anthony Lewis

G. P. PUTNAM'S SONS

AN IMPRINT OF PENGUIN GROUP (USA)

G. P. PUTNAM'S SONS
Published by the Penguin Group
Penguin Group (USA) LLC
375 Hudson Street
New York, NY 10014

USA | Canada | UK | Ireland | Australia
New Zealand | India | South Africa | China
penguin.com
A Penguin Random House Company

Library of Congress Cataloging-in-Publication Data
Coville, Bruce.
Paula Danziger's Amber Brown horses around / written by Bruce Coville
and Elizabeth Levy ; illustrated by Anthony Lewis.
pages cm
Summary: Amber is excited to be spending the summer after fourth grade with
her friends at Camp Cushetunk, but things start getting complicated when she
learns that her worst enemy, Hannah Burton, is one of her bunkmates.
[1. Camps—Fiction. 2. Interpersonal relations—Fiction. 3. Family problems—
Fiction.] I. Levy, Elizabeth, 1942– II. Lewis, Anthony, 1966– illustrator.
III. Danziger, Paula, 1944–2004. IV. Title. V. Title: Amber Brown horses around.
PZ7.C8344Pah 2014
[Fic]—dc23
2013039401

Printed in the United States of America.
ISBN 978-0-399-16170-4
1 3 5 7 9 10 8 6 4 2

Design by Annie Ericsson.
Text set in Bembo.

To Margaret Frith and Susan Kochan,
with love and thanks for watching over
Amber all these years.

SPECIAL THANKS TO:
Kathy Coville, Carrie Danziger, and Ellen Yeomans
for their helpful and heartfelt comments.
The New York Therapeutic Riding Center
for hands-on horse experience.
Annemiek "Mieks" Gersten of Brant Lake Camp
for her insights and advice.
Olivia Fleur Kane for her riding expertise.
Spencer Kane, Houldin and Jonas Marcovitz,
and Isabel and Noah Kirby for patiently answering
questions about life at Amber's age.
Hunter Kane and Julia and Sam Ringel for lots of jokes.

Chapter One

I, Amber Brown, am one happy camper.

This is a strange thing to say, because I have never been at camp . . . . . and I am not there now! Even so, I am a happy camper because I made it through fourth grade and tomorrow I am heading for Camp Cushetunk.

That's the good news.

The bad news is that first I have to pack.

I hate packing. There are too many choices to make!

I am looking at the pile of stuff on my

bed when Mom and Max knock on my door.

I know it is both of them, because the door is open.

I have trained them to knock even when it is.

Max is my new stepfather. I was kind of rotten to him when he started to go out with Mom, but I kind of love him now.

"Come in," I say.

Mom is carrying the packing list that the camp sent. I like lists. I especially like this one because there is a little box next to each item that you can check when you've taken care of it. This is very satisfying.

However, the list is missing things like "Gorilla" and "pig-taking-a-bubble-bath alarm clock/bank." I think I have to leave those things at home. Not because I don't want to have them with me . . . . it's

just that I don't want the other campers to make fun of me for bringing them.

Sometimes it's hard to figure out what is too baby and what is all right.

Max holds up a plastic bag. "I just went to the drugstore, Amber. I think I got everything we still needed."

I thought I liked lists, but I am nothing compared to Max. He LOVES lists.

He also loves labels. I think maybe the two things go together. He has had a fine time ironing name tags onto my shirts and shorts.

I didn't let him do my underwear. I made Mom do that.

When I asked Max how he got so handy with an iron, he explained that it was a side effect of living alone for so many years.

Max starts to unpack the drugstore bag. He holds up a toothbrush. "You're going to love this, Amber. It's got a timer inside and it lights up after you've brushed for two minutes."

Two minutes is how long the dentist wants me to brush, but I usually get bored before two minutes go by. The light is very cool.

Mom says, "Why don't you go grab Amber's towels, Max."

While he is gone, she picks up one of my T-shirts and looks at the name tag. "Amber Brown. I love that I gave you such a colorful name."

I love my name too. But I don't love that Mom's last name is no longer Brown. When she got married to Max, it became Turner.

Max comes back in and puts a stack of towels on the bed. Then he goes to my desk. "Make sure everything has a name tag on it before you pack it."

"I don't think the camp really meant

everything," Mom says. "No one puts a name tag on a tube of toothpaste."

I look at Max and start to laugh. He has a tube of toothpaste in one hand and a fine-point Sharpie in the other. He drops the Sharpie and tries to pretend he wasn't about to label my toothpaste.

"Busted!" I say.

Mom sighs. "Oh, Max. Next thing you know, you'll be labeling her sticks of gum!"

I can't tell whether she is amused or exasperated.

When the trunk is packed, they go downstairs.

"Don't forget we're leaving for the airport in fifteen minutes," Mom calls over her shoulder.

Tonight, Justin Daniels, my very best friend ever, is flying up from Alabama. He is going to Cushetunk too! This is the best, best, best thing ever.

The reason it is the best, best, best thing ever is that I almost never get to see Justin anymore. That's because of one of the worst, worst, worst things ever . . . . his parents moved to Alabama! I thought they should leave Justin behind so we could keep going to school together, but they refused.

Now we're going to be at camp together for four whole weeks. The idea is so exciting, I am afraid my head will explode before we even leave for the airport to get Justin.

I decide to check my e-mail, just to try to keep my head in one piece while I am waiting. I have only had e-mail for a few days . . . . . it was a reward for graduating from fourth grade.

My e-mail name is "Notacrayon."

When I open the account, I see that there is a message from Brandi Colwin. It is addressed to me and Kelly Green.

This is another reason I am so sure Camp Cushetunk will be wonderful. Brandi and Kelly are my best friends from school, and they are going too. It should be great!

Brandi's subject line is "Bulletin! Bulletin! Bulletin!"

She is practicing to be a newscaster, and this is her way of letting Kelly and me know that she has something important to tell us.

I open the e-mail, and groan.

Chapter Two

I don't watch the news that much, but I see it more often now that Max is with us. And something I've noticed is that most of the news is bad.

Brandi's e-mail is definitely something that belongs on the bad news channel.

OMG! I JUST FOUND OUT THAT HANNAH BURTON IS GOING TO CAMP CUSHETUNK!!

I want to beat my head against the keyboard. Hannah and I have been in school together forever, and we have never liked each other.

Hannah Burton is tinfoil on your teeth . . . . . . itching powder down your back . . . . . . a giant booger in your soup.

"What if we're in a bunk with her?" I e-mail back.

Before Brandi can answer, Max calls, "Time to go to the airport!"

I am out of my chair, down the stairs, and into the car while Mom and Max are still getting their things together.

"I checked the flight," Max says as he climbs into the driver's seat. "It's right on time."

It feels like the airport is a million miles away. Every stop sign and traffic light makes me want to scream. I want to be there NOW.

Mom and Max are yakking away like this is just a normal ride. I realize they are talking about the movies they want to see while I am gone. I am not sure I like this . . . . . I think they should just stay home and miss me. I know that is silly, but I can't always control how I feel about things.

When we finally get to the airport, we have to walk a billion zillion miles from the parking garage to where we are supposed to meet Justin. Because he is a kid traveling alone, one of the airplane people will walk him out to us.

I see him! But he is not looking for me. He is chatting away to the woman walking beside him. She is in a uniform and looks very official. She is also very beautiful. For some reason I find this very annoying.

Suddenly he turns in our direction. "Amber!" he cries, and runs toward me. Just like when he came up for Mom and Max's wedding, we almost hug, and then stop.

I look at him. His hair has gotten longer, and he is even more tan than the last
time I saw him. But he is still Justin. Then
he smiles, and I see the big change. He has
braces!

"This is Ms. Block," Justin says. "She's
in training to be a pilot."

Ms. Block shakes hands with Mom and
Max and asks them for ID to make sure
we are the people who are supposed to

pick up Justin. Mom thanks her, and Ms. Block walks away. Justin watches her go.

I tap him on the shoulder. He turns back to me and says, "I think I want to be a pilot when I grow up."

"Come on, flyboy," Max says. "We need to get your luggage."

"Was it scary traveling alone?" I ask Justin.

"No, it was kind of fun. Except they almost paid too much attention to me. But I had my own little TV set. That was cool!"

The luggage comes out on something called a carousel, which would make you think it was like a merry-go-round because it does go around and around. But there aren't any horses. It's a big oval that carries the suitcases and backpacks past the people waiting to claim them. I soooooo want to climb onto it and take a ride . . . . . . I bet it would be fun.

This is when I realize that Max is getting to know me a little too well. He looks down at me and says firmly, "Don't even think about it!"

"That's mine!" Justin says, pointing to a big trunk.

Max hauls it off the carousel. "Ooof! What did you pack in here? Your little brother?"

"I hope he's not in there!" Justin says. "One of the reasons I wanted to go to camp was to get away from him!"

We laugh and head for the car.

When we get home, I say, "Come on, Justin. I'll show you around the new house."

"Great," Mom says. "Max and I will start the grill. We're having a barbecue to celebrate your last night at home before you go to camp."

When we get to my room, I show Justin the place of honor in my closet where I keep our chewing gum ball.

We started making the ball way back in second grade. Justin was going to throw it out when he moved. That started our worst fight ever. I am glad we still have it. It proves that we will always stick together.

"I was afraid your mother might make you throw it away when you were moving," he says.

"She tried," I tell him. "But I stayed strong. Did you bring any gum?"

He shakes his head. "I can't chew gum now that I've got braces. You'll have to chew for both of us."

I pop two pieces into my mouth and chew until they are just right. I add them to the ball, but it's not the same.

"Do the braces hurt?" I ask him. "And how come you didn't tell me you got them?"

He shrugs, which seems to be his answer to both questions. I decide to change the subject. I tell him about Hannah Burton coming to camp.

He doesn't seem half as upset as I am, even though he knows Hannah and doesn't like her either. Instead he says, "I can't believe we'll be at camp tomorrow. I'm dying to swim out to the rock-climbing raft!"

"Rock-climbing raft?" I say. "How can you have a rock-climbing raft in the middle of a lake? It would sink."

"Well, it's not really made of rock, silly. It's inflatable." He looks at my face and says, "What's wrong?"

Instead of answering, I say, "How far is the raft from the dock?"

Justin raises his head just a little. "You don't love swimming, do you?"

He has pretty much read my mind. It is amazing that he can still do this, and it makes me feel good about him as a friend.

But he has not read my whole mind. The truth is, I, Amber Brown, can't swim at all. The divorce happened about the time most of my friends were taking swimming lessons. Somehow the idea of me swimming sank out of sight. If Mom or Dad had suggested lessons, I might have agreed. But since the idea of swimming in water over my head scares me, I never mentioned it myself.

I've managed to keep this secret so far. When I go to the ocean, I squeal and jump in and out of the little waves near the shore. When I am at someone's pool, I hang around in the shallow end and pretend I'm having fun.

I have a feeling that's not going to work at Camp Cushetunk.

I, Amber Brown, realize that part of me is a happy camper and part of me is a scared camper.

And it's not just swimming. Everything is going to be different. And I have never been away from home for so long.

What if I get homesick?

What if camp is not wonderful?

What if I do something stupid and act like a baby?

Suddenly part of me wants to stay home. But it is too late for that.

Tomorrow we leave for Cushetunk.

Chapter
Three

"Amber, it's for you!"

Mom is holding out the phone with one hand and checking her watch with the other.

I take the phone. "Hi, Amber," my father says. "I just wanted to wish you good luck today and tell you again how much I wish that I could be the one driving you and Justin to camp."

He sounds a little miffed about this, which is silly. Justin and I and our two big trunks couldn't fit in his little red sports car, which he calls the Hot Tamale and my mother calls his "Midlife Folly."

"I'm going to miss you so much," he tells me over the phone.

"We can't wait to come up for visiting day."

"We?" I ask.

"Isobel and me," he says, as if it is obvious.

Isobel is Dad's girlfriend. As far as I'm concerned, she is really "Miss Isobel," because that is what we all called her when she was teaching my class ballroom dancing. That's how Dad met her. It was kind of weird when they started dating . . . . but I've gotten used to it now. Even so, I didn't think he would be bringing her to camp.

Camp Cushetunk only has one weekend when the parents are invited. Mom and Dad had to work out which one of them is coming which day. They don't want to be there together. Since Mom and Max get to drive me up, Dad gets the first visiting day. That makes things easier on me, since I won't have to worry about them fighting.

It makes me mad that I have to think about things like that at all. You would think grown-ups could act more . . . . well, grown-up!

"Wait till you see Justin," I tell Dad, partly to change the subject. "He's got braces!"

"I remember my train-track teeth. Tell him not to get too close to any magnets!"

Sometimes my father is not as funny as he thinks he is.

"Write me a letter soon to tell me how your first days go," Dad says.

I'll be writing an old-fashioned letter because the camp doesn't allow e-mail or cell phones. I realize I am going to have to write two letters home each week. Kids like Justin only have to write one.

The divorce was the biggest bad thing

that ever happened. But sometimes it is the little things about it, like worrying about who is going to drive me when, or having to write two letters instead of one, that really bug me. I can feel myself starting to get angry. I don't want to end my last phone call with Dad before camp with a fight, so I tell him I have to go.

"Kissing contest?" he asks.

Immediately I start making kissing sounds.

"No fair!" he cries. "Nobody said GO!" But then he starts making kissy sounds too. Whoever can make the most before our lips give out wins. I know Dad is going to miss me a lot, so even though my lips are getting tired, I keep going.

"You win!" he says at last. "Thanks, Amber. I'll store up those kisses for while you're gone. I'm going to miss you. Have a wonderful time at camp."

After the phone call, Mom makes my favorite breakfast for Justin and me . . . . English muffins with lots of peanut butter and happy faces made out of M&M's.

Max comes into the kitchen. "Can you eat peanut butter with your braces?" he asks Justin. He sounds concerned.

Justin just nods, since he already stuffed a whole muffin face into his mouth.

Max sits. "I've got the car packed and the GPS all programmed."

I'm not used to having someone this organized in my life. Sometimes it is very useful. Sometimes it drives me crazy.

Today, it feels great.

On the drive to camp Max says, "Let's play 'My Grandmother's Trunk.'"

"Your grandmother was an elephant?" Justin says.

"Nice try, funny boy," Max says. "No, it's the game my family always plays on road trips. I start by saying, 'My grand-mother packed a trunk, and in the trunk she put a petunia.' Except it doesn't have to be 'petunia.' Just whatever thing you want to choose. Then the next person has to repeat the sentence, but add a word that starts with the last letter of whatever Gramma just packed.

"Here, let's try it. 'My grandmother packed a trunk, and in the trunk she put an . . . . aardvark.' Over to you, Amber!"

So I have to come up with a word that starts with the last letter of *aardvark*. I choose *kangaroo*. That seems simple. What makes the game tricky is that you have to name everything that came before, so the list keeps getting longer and longer.

When we get to my second turn, I have to remember, "My grandmother packed a trunk, and in the trunk she put an aardvark, a kangaroo, an opal . . . . a lolli-pop, a pickle, and an elephant."

Justin says, "My grandmother packed a trunk, and in the trunk she put an aardvark, a kangaroo, an opal, a lollipop, a pickle, an elephant, and the *Titanic*."

"How big is this trunk, anyway?" Mom asks, laughing.

Actually we are all laughing.

My mother misses on the next round. I have a feeling Max could keep going forever. It's that organized brain thing.

About halfway to camp we stop for ice cream. I get pistachio. Justin says it should be called "booger" because of the color. That doesn't stop him from doing what we always used to do when we got ice cream . . . . pushing the cones together so I get some of his chocolate and he gets some of my pistachio. You have to do this very carefully. Otherwise your ice cream ends up on the ground.

Justin and I know this from sad experience.

Max decides that ice-cream mashing looks like fun, but when he tries to get Mom to do it, she rolls her eyes and says, "Taking a trip with you and those two is like traveling with three kids." But then she gives him a kiss to let him know she doesn't really mean it.

"Kisses are better than ice cream," Max says.

After we wash our faces . . . mine is chocolate colored on one side and green on the other . . . we pile back into the car.

We are having so much fun playing "My Grandmother's Trunk" that we almost don't hear the GPS tell us we are only four miles from camp.

I have been concentrating so hard on the game, I haven't been paying much attention to the countryside. Now I see that we are in a very green and hilly area. Off to our right is a hill so high, I think it might be a mountain. This makes me wonder how big a hill has to be before it gets to be called a mountain. Do little hills want to be mountains when they grow up?

Sometimes even I think that the things I think are silly!

"Welcome to Camp Cushetunk!" Justin shouts. He is pointing to a sign made from birch tree branches.

We drive up a long hill, through tall pine trees. When we come to a clearing, we see posters directing us where to park.

As we get out of the car, a woman dressed in shorts and a blue Camp Cushetunk polo shirt comes over to greet us. She is holding a clipboard and has a whistle around her neck. "My name is Miss Flo," she says. "I'm the camp director." She looks at me carefully, then says, "Amber, right?"

"How did you know?" I ask.

She smiles. "You and your parents sent a picture with your application, remember?"

Max looks at Miss Flo with admiration. "Do you mean you already know the name of every camper?"

Miss Flo nods. "It's kind of a game for me, but I also believe it makes the campers happy that we know who they are."

"And I thought 'My Grandmother's Trunk' was a challenge," Max says.

"You're Justin Daniels," Miss Flo continues. "We love getting second generations. I remember your parents well." She smiles. "Maybe someday I'll tell you a story about your father and mother. Anyway, you'll be in Pete's cabin. He's one of the waterfront counselors. I think you'll get along great. He's from Minnesota, the Land of Lakes, so they've been dunking him since he was no bigger than a minnow."

I'm kind of wishing I was a minnow myself. Then I would have been born knowing how to swim.

Miss Flo turns to me. "Amber, you'll be with Carrie from Kiev."

I know where Minnesota is, but I've never heard of Kiev.

"Isn't that far to come?" Mom asks.

"We have counselors from all over the world. It's part of the Cushetunk Experience. Carrie is our riding instructor. She

29

was riding before she could walk. She was on the Ukrainian national team."

Now I have two things to be nervous about . . . . . swimming and horseback riding. Unless you count the pony ride Aunt Pam took me on once at the zoo, I've never been anywhere near a horse.

"Are your trunks labeled?" Miss Flo asks.

If she knew Max, she wouldn't have to ask.

"*Everything* is labeled," Mom says.

Max grins. He is sure he is getting a compliment.

"Good," Miss Flo says. "Just leave your trunks here. We'll have them delivered to your bunks. We call it 'trunk to bunk' service." She turns to Mom and Max. "And now it's time for parental units to say good-bye."

She is smiling, but it is plain that she wants them to clear out.

Mom gives Justin a big hug. Then she reaches for me and holds me tight. I look up at her. She has tears in her eyes. "Have a fabulous time, Amber." She smiles. "We'll be sending a package for your birthday." She digs in her purse for a tissue. After she wipes her nose, she says, "I can't believe I won't be with you when you turn ten!"

Max wipes away a tear too. "I'll miss you, you little monkey." He has never called me a little monkey before. It's kind of sweet. I'll just have to make sure he doesn't do it all the time.

A tall, tan teenager comes over and says, "Hey, Justin. I'm Pete. Let's go to the flagpole."

Someone taps me on the shoulder. I turn around and see a counselor with red hair and big blue eyes. She says, "You're Amber, right? I'm Carrie."

"From Kiev," I answer.

"You'll be in my cabin," Carrie says. "It's the best bunk. You'll see."

"Your English is so good," I tell her.

She smiles again. "Thank you. I went to the American School in Kiev."

We walk to the flagpole.

I hear a squeal. Kelly and Brandi come running over to hug me.

When we are done squealing and hugging, Carrie says, "Come on, Amber, let's get you settled in. You'll see your friends again at dinner."

"Don't worry," Kelly says. "I checked it out. We're only one cabin over."

That's when I realize the terrible truth . . . I'm going to be in a different bunk than Brandi and Kelly! It didn't even occur to me to worry about this. I just always thought we would be together.

Carrie takes me to a path that winds into the forest. It leads to a wooden building.

"Ta-da!" she says. "Your home for the next four weeks."

She flings open the door. Standing at one of the bunks, their backs to us, are three girls. When they hear the door open, they turn to face us.

As they move aside, I can see a fourth girl. It is clear that the other girls had been gathered around her, as if she was already their leader.

My heart sinks.

My stomach clenches.

My toes curl.

I wonder if it is too late to go home. Because if it is, I'm going to have to spend the next four weeks sharing a cabin with Hannah Burton.

Chapter
Four

"Oh, look," Hannah says. "It's Amber Brown, the world's only living crayon!"

"Hannah," Carrie warns. "We have a rule at Camp Cushetunk. No put-downs. Girls, you are all bunkmates. I expect you to have each other's backs."

Hannah glares at me as if what she wants to do with my back is put a dagger in it.

Putting a hand on my shoulder, Carrie says, "Hannah, I know you and Amber go

to school together. Why don't you introduce her to the other girls?"

Hannah sighs and says, "Amber, this is
Treasure Jackson." She is pointing to a tall
black girl.

"Hi, Amber," Treasure says. "Welcome
to Camp Cushetunk. I was here last year.
You'll love it."

I notice that she has a great smile.

"Treasure is sleeping in my upper
bunk," Hannah says, as if wanting it to
be clear that Treasure is going to be her
friend, not mine.

The girl next to Treasure doesn't wait
for Hannah. "I'm Shannon Cohn." She
holds her hand out and starts toward me.
She doesn't really walk, she kind of
bounces. So does her curly red hair. She
shakes my hand.

"I'm Grace Anderson," the third girl
says. She is about my height but a lot

thicker than I am. I don't mean that she is fat, just that she looks strong. I can tell that she is by the fact that my hand hurts when she shakes it.

"I have to go," Carrie says. "I've still got one more camper to meet."

I feel a little panicked . . . . I want to tell Carrie not to leave me here. I don't know how to explain it. The whole time I was excited about going to camp, I kind of thought of it as a time to be with Brandi,

Kelly, and Justin without having to worry about school. I can't believe I forgot there would be so many kids here that I had never met.

There is only one bunk left, and I get to choose whether I want the upper or lower bed. This is something else I haven't thought about. I don't know whether to pick top or bottom. I feel like I'm a molar trying to decide where to live.

Treasure comes over and says, "Most

kids like the bottom bunk because it's easier to get up to go pee. Also, people hang out on the bottom bunks. I like to hang out, but not all the time. On top it's kind of private, and it's fun. You can flop over the edge and watch people sleep. People are pretty funny when they're sleeping."

Hannah looks annoyed. I can't tell if it's because Treasure is talking to me, or because Hannah has suddenly decided she should have taken a top bunk instead.

"I think I want the top," I say. I practice climbing up. Treasure was right. It's fun. There is a window and it feels like being in a tree house. I'm really glad I chose the top.

Just then, Carrie comes back in. She has an Asian-looking girl with her.

"Ladies, meet Cleo Wu," Carrie says. "Now our bunk is complete."

"Hi, Cleo," I say quickly, hanging my

head over the edge of the mattress. "I'm Amber."

I feel very good that I manage to do this before Hannah can say anything. I smile at Cleo, but then worry that it looks like a frown, since my head is upside down. I clamber to the floor and hold out my hand. Cleo takes it, and we shake.

"Have you been here before?" she asks.

"Nope. Treasure has, though." I point in her direction.

Grace leaps up. "I was here last year too. I'm Grace Anderson."

Shannon smiles at Cleo. "I'm new like you. Shannon Cohn."

"How about you?" Cleo points to Hannah.

"It's my first time." Hannah looks very put out. "But I don't feel new. I know all about Camp Cushetunk because my parents both came here when they were kids."

I didn't know this. It annoys me, but I can't figure out why. Maybe it's because every conversation with Hannah seems to turn into some sort of contest while I'm not looking.

Someone knocks at the door. Carrie pulls it open. "Ah, we have achieved trunkage! Haul them in, gentlemen. Kids, your stuff is here. Most of your things should stay in your trunk. Treasure and Grace, show them how we do it."

We have cubbies, which makes me think of kindergarten. Our trunks go in the bottom, then there is a shelf, and then a few pegs to hang things on.

Getting unpacked doesn't take long.

Carrie blows a whistle. When we come running over, she is smiling. "I love doing that," she says. "Come on, let's head for chow."

I wonder if we are going to have to

walk in a line, but we end up looking more like a cluster of ducklings following their mother. I am walking next to Cleo. She starts telling me lightbulb jokes.

My favorite is, "How many campers does it take to change a lightbulb?"

The answer is, "It depends on how big the flashlight is."

I think I am going to like her.

When we enter the mess hall I get nervous. The place is huge! I am feeling a bit lost when Carrie comes up to Cleo and me. "At Cushetunk we sit at assigned tables," she tells us. "But we change the table mix every week. That way, you get to meet almost everyone. But you start with your own age group."

She shows us to a seating chart posted on the wall. I almost shriek when I find my name. I am at a table with Justin, Kelly, and Treasure, plus a few other people that

I don't know. I'm sorry I'm not with Brandi, but overjoyed that I'm not with Hannah.

I secretly bless Miss Flo for putting me with Justin for this first week. She must have remembered what I wrote in my essay . . . . . one reason I wanted to come to Cushetunk was so that Justin and I could spend the summer together.

Justin is already at the table. He grins at me. I still can't get used to his braces. He is with his counselor, Pete. I get to sit next to Justin. Perfect!

"How's it going?" Justin asks. "My bunk is great."

"My bunk has Hannah in it," I whisper to him. Well, actually I kind of growl it.

Before I can say more, Pete interrupts. He makes us all introduce ourselves. When we are done, he says, "We have lots of traditions at Camp Cushetunk, and the first-night dinner is one of my favorites.

As counselor for your table, I get to pick the question."

"Question?" I ask. "Like what do we want to eat?"

"No," he says. "The menu is already settled. The question for the table is, 'How would the world be different if animals could talk?'"

"Well, if they were zebras, they would say, 'I want a little color in my life!'" I call out.

"I think the animals would say, 'You humans aren't half as smart as you think you are,'" Justin says.

"Oh, Justin," Treasure says. "You're right! I think animals are so much smarter than anyone knows."

Justin blushes. But he is smiling.

Nobody seems to like my idea . . . . . and now I am sorry that I made a stupid joke. Soon everyone is talking about his or her favorite animal, and why it is so smart. I realize I don't really have a favorite animal, except Gorilla, but I'm afraid someone will laugh if I name him.

"Nobody picked a mule," Treasure says. She laughs and starts to sing a song about a mule.

"You've got a great voice," Pete tells her.

Justin nods. "My parents like to sing that song."

"It's a Cushetunk favorite," Pete says.

Treasure smiles. "Speaking of favorites, everybody ready for s'mores? It's a first-campfire tradition."

Justin grins. "I love s'mores!"

"Cushetunk s'mores are the best," Treasure says.

Soon we are heading outdoors to the campfire area. It is wonderful, a half circle on the hillside overlooking the lake. On the beach is a big pile of wood shaped like a teepee. We sit on the ground facing the pile of wood, and applaud as the counselors light the fire.

Justin grins at me. "My parents said the campfires were their favorite thing at Cushetunk."

When the fire is blazing away, three counselors teach us the Camp Cushetunk anthem.

Cushetunk, Cushetunk,
We will never forsake you.
Hills of green,
Shores serene,
And your waters of clear blue.
Home of our hearts
You will always be,
No matter where we wander.
Cushetunk, Cushetunk,
Our hearts grow ever fonder!

We sing it again at the end of the campfire. I am so happy. The sky is dark and I can see more stars than I even knew existed. The air is as sweet as the s'mores. Treasure was right. I am going to love it here.

Chapter Five

I, Amber Brown, am one unhappy camper. I am standing on the dock in my swimsuit. I am shivering . . . . not just because it's morning and it's cold. I'm shivering because it's our bunk's turn for the swimming test.

Pete blows a whistle. "Listen up, campers! We'll be testing two people at a time. Jump in and start swimming. You can use any stroke, just do what you can. Remember, it takes eight laps to be certified for the climbing rock."

I am at the back of the line. What am I going to do? I can't jump in the deep water. But I don't want to admit in front of everyone that I can't swim.

Grace is standing in front of me. "Did you know this is the deepest lake in New Jersey?"

I shake my head. I didn't know that, and I wish I still didn't know it. But now that I do know, how can I forget it?

Hannah and Cleo are at the front of the line. Hannah makes a perfect dive. Cleo just jumps. They both swim eight laps with no problem.

Treasure and Shannon go next. Treasure does eight laps but Shannon gives up after six. Pete tells her that she'll be in the Guppy group, and she should be able to do the full eight by next week.

Now Grace and I are at the edge of the dock. Grace jumps in. I just stand there.

"Go ahead, Amber," Pete says.

"I can't do it," I whisper.

"Not at all?" he asks. "Not even one lap?"

I shake my head. I am trying not to cry, but I am really, really embarrassed. It doesn't help that I can hear Hannah snickering somewhere behind me.

Pete puts a hand on my shoulder. "No problem," he says. "I am going to have you swimming like a Minnesota minnow before you know it."

"Don't worry, Amber," Hannah calls from the edge of the dock. "When we go fishing, you can be the sinker."

Pete blows his whistle. "Put-down violation! Off the dock, Hannah. Go sit on the beach."

Hannah glares at me, then flounces off the dock.

After the swimming test, we head for the bunk to change for our first visit to the riding rink. Carrie told us at breakfast that the rule for the stables is no shorts and no sandals.

I am still embarrassed about not being able to swim. What if horseback riding is the same way and everybody except me already knows how to do it?

When I said I wanted to go to camp, I didn't realize how many new things I was going to have to try!

As we head for the horses, Hannah links

arms with Treasure and Grace. She has not spoken to me since swimming, which is fine.

Six horses, already saddled, are waiting in the ring. They are tied to the fence. Carrie is in the middle of the ring. She has on riding boots that come up to her knees. She is also wearing a helmet. I think bicycle helmets are ugly, but this helmet is actually cute.

"You kids are lucky," Carrie tells us as she passes out helmets. "Camp Cushetunk has a long riding tradition. We have some wonderful and well-trained horses for you to get to know."

"They're awfully big," I say.

I already knew horses are big . . . . . but I hadn't realized how big until we were standing right in front of them.

Carrie puts her hand on the neck of one of the horses. "Amber, let's get you started on Cinnamon."

Unlike me, Cinnamon actually is the same color as her name. I expect Hannah to make some joke about this, but she is standing at the back of the group, looking nervous.

"You're going to love Cinnamon," Carrie tells me. "She's a sweetheart. Put your helmet on and come meet her."

I look at Cinnamon. She has a white blaze on her forehead. It's pretty, and she may be a sweetheart, but the way she is switching her tail back and forth makes me nervous.

Carrie gestures to me. I strap on the helmet and walk over. Carrie takes my hand and tells me to let Cinnamon smell it.

"She won't bite?" I ask.

Carrie smiles. "No. I told you, she's a sweetie."

Next, Carrie lifts my hand and puts it on Cinnamon's neck. It is warm and smooth.

"Riders always mount from the left," Carrie says. She cups her hands. "Give me your foot."

"Right now?" I ask. "Don't Cinnamon and I have to get to know each other better first?"

"You'll get to know each other from the saddle. That's where the rider belongs . . . . . on top. Hold on to the saddle with both hands."

I stretch up. My fingertips just reach the saddle.

"Foot!" Carrie orders.

I give her my left foot.

"Up you go!"

Somehow, without even knowing what I'm doing, I swing my right leg around, and all at once I'm in the saddle. But I'm not sitting . . . . . I've tipped forward and my face has fallen on Cinnamon's mane. It isn't nearly as soft as her neck. In fact, it's kind of prickly.

I push myself back up.

"Great!" Carrie adjusts my stirrups. "Now pat Cinnamon and tell her sweet nothings while I get the other kids mounted."

It's awfully high up, but I can see all the way across the meadow. I decide to tell Cinnamon that. "You have a nice view," I say, patting her neck. She nods. Is she listening to me?

Carrie is busy getting the other girls on their horses. Hannah goes last, and she looks really unhappy.

"It's a long way to the ground," she complains to Carrie.

"Good reason to stay in the saddle," Carrie answers.

This is the first time I have seen Hannah act as if she didn't think she could do something better than everyone else.

The idea makes me kind of happy. That makes me feel a little guilty.

"Well, I can't be nice all the time," I whisper to Cinnamon.

She nods again.

I think I am going to love her.

Chapter Six

Dear Dad,

You wanted me to tell you about the first days of camp, so here goes. First off, I like the camp and I like my bunkmates, mostly. I also like our counselor, "Carrie from Kiev."

What I don't like is the fact that I am a "Polliwog." That's what they call the group for kids who can't swim at all. I have to stay in a roped-off area called the Polliwog Pond until I learn to swim.

That's the bad news.

The good news is that I have a "natural seat." You probably didn't think I had an artificial bottom anyway, but a natural seat means that I am a natural on a horse.

Oh, Dad! I can't tell you how much I love it! The horse I ride is named Cinnamon, and when I am on her back I feel tall and strong. I have had three riding lessons so far, and they are the best, best, best part of camp. Well, actually Justin being here is the best, best, best part of camp. But this is almost as good.

I hope you are doing all right without me. Ha Ha. Please tell Miss Isobel I said hello, and pat Mewkiss Membrane for me.

Your loving daughter,

Amber

PS: Do you suppose that I could have a horse for Christmas??

PPS: Only kidding.

PPPS: Or maybe not . . .

Chapter Seven

BOOM!

That is the sound of a huge burst of thunder.

"Aaaaaah!" This is the sound of Cleo screaming.

Treasure laughs. "Relax, Cleo, this is fun!"

"I agree," Grace says. "I think lightning is *excit'ning*."

I like thunderstorms too. But a thunderstorm when you are safe in your own home is very different from a thunder-storm when you are in a small cabin in the woods . . . . . especially at night.

We hear a sizzle of lightning, and the cabin goes dark. It's not lights-out . . . . . . well, yes, the lights do go out. But not because it is time for bed.

"It's okay, everybody," Carrie says. "It's just a power outage." She lights a lantern. Holding it up to her face, she adds, "I think this is a good night for a story."

"YAY!" we all shout.

"Okay, gather 'round."

We sit in a circle on the floor. Carrie perches on Hannah's bunk. She looks at the door, then back at us. "You have to promise not to tell anyone about this."

"Why?" Hannah asks.

Carrie lowers her voice. "Because I'm about to tell you something I shouldn't. So it's silence, okay?"

We all nod.

Carrie smiles and dims the lantern so there's just a little glow around her.

As the wind howls outside the cabin, she says, "I'm going to tell you the story of the Lake Cushetunk Monster."

"Cushie, the demon of the deep!" Treasure and Grace say in unison.

Carrie nods. "The camp doesn't like us to talk about Cushie."

"Why?" Hannah asks.

Treasure rolls her eyes. "Because it would be bad for business, obviously! Stop interrupting!"

"All right, you know how deep Lake Cushetunk is?" Carrie says.

"The deepest lake in New Jersey," Cleo murmurs. She sounds a little scared.

"Yes," Carrie says in a low, spooky voice, "the deepest. And in the deepest recess of this deep, deep lake, out near the climbing raft, Cushie was born. The last of her species . . . . . lonely . . . . ah, so alone . . . . . until humans came to the edge of her lake. And so Cushie began to think perhaps these creatures who came to her lake's edge . . . perhaps they could be her friends. But can humans become friends with a monster?"

Carrie holds the lantern close to her face and shakes her head. "Yet every summer, a camper is chosen, a camper just like you. Cushie takes you to the deep, and when you return to us . . . . ah . . . . . you still look human, but your heart has been changed, and you will forever hunger for the deep, yearn to re-turn to those dark, cold waters." She drops her voice to a whisper. "And there is always the danger that you will want to drag another camper down to Cushie's lair with you, down into those dark, cold waters."

"Is there any way to know who this has

happened to?" Hannah asks. I have never heard her sound so small and timid.

Carrie nods. "They say . . . I don't know this for sure, because I've never seen it . . . but they say that on the night of the full moon, a strange oozing appears on the chosen one's face."

"Half human, half Cushetunk Monster!" Treasure says.

"A Cushetunk zombie," Grace cries.

"Well, I didn't say that," Carrie says.

Hannah crosses her arms. "You made this all up. There is no Cushetunk Monster."

Treasure snorts. "That's what newbies always say."

"My parents never talked about the Cushetunk Monster," Hannah insists.

"We're all sworn not to talk about it outside of camp," Grace tells her.

Carrie nods.

Just then, the lights go back on.

Carrie turns off her lantern. "Well, kids,

it's time for real lights-out. Wash up and get into bed." She looks at the chart on the wall. "Hannah, you're first tonight."

"Careful the Cushie Monster doesn't get you," Grace warns. "They say it can send something up through the drain that will make you long to go to the water's edge so it can take you."

"The Cushie Monster is not real," Hannah says. To my surprise, I hear a little tremble in her voice.

I am last into the bathroom that night. I see Hannah whispering to Treasure when I hang up my towel.

As I climb into my bed, Carrie says, "Last camper is in her bunk. Lights out!"

I put my head down on my pillow. I feel something sticky and wet on my cheek. I sit up so fast, I hit my head on the ceiling. I put my hand to my cheek. It is gooey and slimy. "Yuck! Yuck!" I cry.

Carrie hurries to my bed. She shines

her flashlight on my face, runs a finger over my cheek, then raises it to her nose and takes a sniff. She sighs. "Okay, girls, whoever put the hair gel on Amber's pillowcase, it's not funny!" She turns to me. "I'll be right back."

She goes into the bathroom. When she comes back, she has a wet washcloth and helps me clean my face. Then she gets me a new pillowcase. Once that's done, she says loudly, "I don't want any more of that stuff, you guys. Understand?"

There is a long silence.

"Understand?" Carrie repeats, and this time she sounds very stern.

"Yes, Carrie," everyone replies.

"All right, then let's get some sleep. We've got another big day tomorrow." She pauses. "Besides, it's a well-known fact that it's easier to resist Cushie if you get all the rest you need."

She goes behind the wall to where her own bunk is. I'm not sure, but I think I can hear her chuckling to herself.

Cleo pokes my mattress. "Are you okay, Amber?" she whispers.

I lean my head down. "Did you see who messed with my pillow?"

"No, I was hiding under the covers. I don't like thunderstorms." Cleo waits a second, then says, "Do you think the Cushie Monster is real?"

"No," I say. I like Cleo, and I don't want her to be scared.

"I didn't think so. But I wanted your opinion. I'm sorry about your pillow. I don't know who would be mean enough to do that."

I do, I think. I know exactly who would be that nasty.

Hannah Burton.

Chapter Eight

"Okay, faces in the water!"

That's Pete speaking. The good thing about being a Polliwog is that twice a day I get a semiprivate swimming lesson from Pete . . . . . or "Pete-the-Hunk," as some of the older girls call him. It's semiprivate because there is one other non-swimmer in our age group, a kid named Colin. He's from New York City and is in Justin's bunk. I know that Justin likes him, so that makes him okay with me.

The bad thing is that I have to keep putting my face in the water. Well, it was bad to begin with. But I'm getting used to it, so that's progress. Colin still kind of hates it. I feel a little sorry for him.

Pete says that the reason he keeps having us put our faces in the water is so we'll get comfortable with it. When we lift our heads, he says, "Well done, my favorite Polliwogs!"

"We're your only Polliwogs," Colin points out.

"That's why you're my favorites," Pete says. "Now, this is a big day . . . . . we're going to try your elementary backstroke in the water."

The reason Pete says we're going to try the elementary backstroke in the water is that for the last couple of days we've been doing it on the sand. This isn't the regular backstroke you see on the Olympics . . . . that would lead to a lot of holes on the beach.

First we slide our hands up our sides.

Pete calls this the "tickle your armpits" move. Then we stretch our arms out and sweep them back toward the starting position. At the same time we do a frog kick, which is pretty much what you would think.

It's kind of like making sand angels, which is fun. And sand will always hold you up . . . . . unless it's quicksand, which this isn't. But the idea of doing this in the lake with my feet off the bottom is almost as scary as quicksand.

"You first, Amber," Pete says. He has me float on my back. As I do, he puts his arms underneath me to support me. "Okay, go," he says.

To my surprise, doing this in water is easier than I imagined. I'm actually moving. And with Pete staying beside me, I'm not scared.

"Great, Amber!" Pete says.

I do two more strokes.

And then I realize that though Pete is there to catch me, he isn't really holding me up. I am floating and moving on my own.

I, Amber Brown, am swimming!!!

After a minute, Pete stops me and says, "Look, you did half a lap!"

I really did. Yay, me!

Pete and I wade back to Colin.

"You were amazing!" Colin tells me.

I grin at him. "Your turn now. It's easy. You'll see."

Colin wraps his arms around his chest. He looks scared. But Pete leads him out a little deeper. With Pete's support, Colin floats on his back. Soon he is moving through the water the way I did.

As Colin wades back to me, he has a big grin on his face. We give each other a high five.

"Your turn again, Amber," Pete calls. "Come on out."

Soon I am floating again. I know Pete's hand is there to keep me safe, but his touch is so light I can barely feel it. On my back I move through the water. I can look up and see the whole sky stretching out over me. Cool!

Just as I am feeling really confident, someone calls, "Wow, Amber, that's great!"

I turn toward the voice and that's when it happens. I breathe in when I shouldn't and get a noseful of water.

It's horrible! I cough and gasp and start to sink. I am terrified, but Pete is fast. He gets me on my feet right away.

I want to clobber whoever it was that called to me, but when I turn toward the dock, I see that it was Justin. I am so embarrassed that he saw me goof up. But he wasn't the only one. Treasure is standing on the dock beside him.

"Don't worry, Amber," she says. "You'll get it next time."

I don't know why, but I don't like her saying that.

I don't know why, but I don't like the way she and Justin are standing together.

I don't know why, but I have a terrible knot in my stomach.

Chapter
Nine

Dear Mom and Max,
  The package arrived!
  It's sooooo big!!! I can't wait to find out what's in it!! I know part of it will be some treats to eat. I also know that Miss Flo told you if you send goodies you have to send enough for me to share with everyone in my age group. But I can't wait to find out what else might be in there!
  Oh! Did Miss Flo tell you WHERE I get to share the treats??

ON THE BIRTHDAY BOAT TRIP!

Anyone who has a birthday during camp gets to go out on the party boat with all the kids in her age group. That means I get to go with Justin, Brandi, Kelly, and all the other neat kids I've been telling you about in my letters, like Treasure and Colin.

It does mean that Hannah Burton comes too . . . . . which is sort of an UNbirthday present. I told you that she's in my bunk. She's as much of a pain as ever, but camp is so great I almost don't mind her.

Too bad I can't bring Cinnamon. The boat is big, but not big enough for a horse. I'm going to save one of the treats and give it to her.

Official Notice! I, Amber Brown, am going to be double digits tomorrow. I've been waiting almost ten years for this!

So here's ten kisses!
X X X X X X X X X X

Love from your little bundle of joy,

Amber

Chapter Ten

"Wake up, little Amber, wake up!"

Why would anyone be singing to me first thing in the morning? The camp's idea of an alarm clock is a bugle playing through the loudspeaker, not singing.

I open my eyes and see Carrie and all my bunkmates gathered below me. As soon as I sit up, they shout, "Happy birthday!" Someone has tied red and yellow balloons to the corners of my bunk.

"This is how we do birthdays at Camp Cushetunk," Carrie tells me.

"Yeah," Hannah says. "We had to get up a full half hour early just for you."

Treasure starts singing "Happy Birthday." Everyone joins her, ignoring Hannah. When they get to "Happy birthday, dear Amber," they shower me with glitter.

I decide I like the Camp Cushetunk style.

"You are so lucky to have a summer birthday," Grace says.

I never felt lucky before. I usually don't like having a July birthday because school is out and a lot of my friends aren't around. But this is great.

Carrie goes into her room and comes out with the package from Mom and Max, and another one that came from Dad. There's a third box that must have just arrived. I bet it's from Aunt Pam. Her presents are always the funniest.

"Camp tradition says that birthday kids

open their presents before breakfast," Carrie tells me.

This is the most sensible rule I have heard in a long time.

The package from Mom and Max is heavy. I tear it open and find a huge box of homemade cookies with M&M's in them. Taped to the cookie box is a big sign in Max's handwriting . . . . . NUT FREE.

"That's right," Carrie says. "The only nuts in this camp are the kids in my bunk."

We all throw pillows at her.

The heavy part of Mom and Max's present turns out to be a box of books. I can tell they are books by their shapes. But I don't know what books they are, because each one is wrapped separately.

"Boy, your mom is a whiz at wrapping," Shannon says.

I smile. "No, Max did this. I can tell because the corners are so neat."

"Who's Max?" Grace asks. "Your brother?"

"No, my stepfather."

I am startled when I say this. I realize it is the first time I have called Max my stepfather out loud. It makes me kind of wish he was here so I could give him a hug.

The first book I unwrap is *The Black Stallion*.

"Oh, that's my favorite," Carrie says. "I used it to learn English."

By the time I am done unwrapping the books, it's clear that Mom and Max must have paid attention when I wrote to them about how much I love riding Cinnamon. Every one of them is a horse book! I can't wait to start reading them.

I decide to open Aunt Pam's present next. I want to save Dad's for last.

"I love that wrapping paper," Cleo says.

"Dancing hippos are Aunt Pam's style," I tell her.

Under the paper is a medium-size box. I open it carefully, then burst out laughing.

"What is it?" Grace demands.

"Pooping reindeer!" I cry, holding up a box so they can see the label.

Hannah makes a face. "That's disgusting."

"Are you kidding?" Treasure says. "It's hilarious. See? It poops little brown candies."

"My aunt Pam is the queen of goofy gifts," I say. "And she sent one for each of you!"

The girls cheer.

The "enough treats for everyone" rule is really about food, but Aunt Pam is the kind who would make it apply to presents too. Even better, when I get to the bottom of the box, I see an extra reindeer. On it is a yellow stickie that says, "For Justin."

I love Aunt Pam.

Everyone thinks the pooping reindeer are a riot. Well, everyone but Hannah, but she takes hers anyway.

While my bunkmates are figuring out how to load the candies into the reindeer and then get them to poop out, I open the present from Dad.

It is the smallest box, but as Mom used to tell me when I was really little, sometimes good things come in small packages. That is definitely true in this case. Under the wrapping paper is a velvety blue box. Inside is a silver horseshoe on a delicate silver chain. It is decorated with tiny clear stones that sparkle in the morning light.

Tucked into the lid of the box is a folded-up piece of paper. It is a note from Dad.

Dear Amber—
Ten years ago you made me the
happiest man on Earth by being born.
I still feel that way. On this horseshoe,
which is a sign of good luck, are ten tiny
diamonds, to celebrate ten wonderful
years of having the best daughter
possible. Happy birthday to my girl.

Love,
Dad

I climb down from the bunk to look in the mirror.

"That's so beautiful," Cleo says as I put the chain around my neck.

"I'm never taking it off," I say. "Horse-shoes are good luck."

When we get to the mess hall, I go to Justin's table to give him his pooping reindeer.

"Let me guess," he says. "Aunt Pam?"

I smile. "Naturally."

Then I show Justin the necklace.

"It's pretty," Colin says.

"I've got M&M cookies for everybody on the boat ride," I say.

"I've got a present for you too," Justin says. He hands me something wrapped in aluminum foil. I wonder if he got his bunkmates to chew up some gum for our chewing gum ball, but when I open the foil, I find a lariat key chain.

"I made it myself," Justin tells me. "It's for the keys for your new house."

"Thank you," I say. "I love it."

I kind of want to hug him, but it would feel weird in front of everyone. Or maybe just plain weird. We haven't hugged each other since we were really little. I wonder how come it was okay for us to hug back then. I wonder why we stopped when we got older. I wonder if I will ever figure this stuff out.

I hear a familiar voice come over the loudspeaker. "Bulletin! Bulletin! Bulletin! This is WCTK, your friendly camp radio, coming to you live with an important announcement."

Brandi loves getting to work on the camp radio program, which broadcasts our announcements every morning from a booth off the mess hall.

"TODAY IS MY FRIEND AMBER BROWN'S BIRTHDAY! So I am wishing her a big happy, happy birthday. Amber Brown is a most colorful character and a great friend."

I blush. Then Brandi comes out of the radio booth and gives me a hug.

The entire camp sings "Happy Birthday" to me.

This is so cool. And it's even before the boat ride!

"All right, everyone," Pete calls. "Make sure your life jackets are fastened before you get on the boat."

"I hate wearing a life jacket," Hannah mutters. "They just look so clunky, and I can swim perfectly well."

As far as I am concerned, if Hannah doesn't wear a life jacket, that is just fine. But I know the camp will not allow it.

I promise Brandi and Kelly that I will sit next to them on the boat. They can help me pass out the cookies from Mom and Max.

There are seats all around the edges of the boat. Toward the front is a raised area where the controls are. Miss Flo is sitting there. "Welcome aboard, Amber!" she calls. "Happy birthday!"

Last to board is Pete. "That's it," he shouts. "Twenty-four of Cushetunk's finest campers, all secure and ready to go."

Two other counselors are on the dock. They untie the boat. Miss Flo revs the engine and we're off!

I love this ride! Sometimes it is a little bumpy, but that's part of the fun. At first we stay fairly close to shore, but when we are about halfway around the lake, Miss Flo turns the boat toward the center. Then she switches off the engine. It is nice to have it so quiet.

It's time to share my treats. Brandi and Kelly help me pass them out.

"I wonder if the Cushie Monster would like one of these," Brandi says.

"Yeah!" Justin says. "I bet that the Cushie Monster loves M&M's."

"I've heard that the Cushie Monster only likes s'mores," Kelly says.

"Your bunk knows about the Cushie Monster?" I ask. "Carrie told us it's a secret."

"I don't think you should talk about it," Hannah says. "Aren't we in the deepest part of the lake?"

"Yes." Treasure giggles. "The very deepest." She breaks off part of a cookie and

throws it into the lake. "This is for you, Cushie!"

The cookie makes a plop as it hits the water.

"Don't do that!" Hannah cries.

We hear another splash, and I see that a big fish has risen to the surface. It gulps down the piece of cookie.

"Look!" I gasp. "I think that was one of the Cushie Monster's tentacles."

"That's not funny!" Hannah snaps.

"You want funny?" Colin asks. "That reindeer your aunt gave Justin is the funniest thing I've ever seen."

Kelly and Brandi snort when I tell them about the pooping reindeer. "I'll have Aunt Pam send some for you for Christmas," I promise.

Hannah is glaring at me as if she doesn't like pooping reindeer, she doesn't like the talk about Cushie, she doesn't like Justin and Colin laughing with me, she doesn't like that Brandi and Kelly are laughing too. She doesn't like me.

I don't care. I finger my horseshoe. I feel very lucky.

Chapter
Eleven

Dear Aunt Pam,

*Your pooping reindeer were a big hit!
Thank you, thank you, thank you!
All four bunks in my age group have
decided that you are the coolest aunt in
the universe. I already knew that, of
course.*

*Did you ever go to camp? I bet you
were everyone's favorite camper. Did
you do pranks? They seem to happen a
lot around here. One night, someone
put hair gel on my pillow . . . . . it
really scared me because we had been*

talking about the Cushetunk Monster and I thought it was slime! I am pretty sure that Hannah Burton . . . . you remember, Little Miss Perfect who's not so perfect . . . . . did that one.

Brandi and Kelly told me that someone in their bunk brought itching powder. They say that itchy isn't that funny.

One day when my bunk got up, someone had taken everyone's socks and put one sock from each pair in a scrambled pile in the middle of the floor. It took us half an hour to find the other socks . . . . they were in a big laundry bag, hanging from a tree about ten feet from our cabin. That one was annoying, but it was also kind of funny. Since it happened to all of us, I don't think it was any of the kids in our bunk who did it. Secretly I suspect it was our counselor, Carrie. She is wonderful, but I think she likes mischief. Maybe she thought that working together to rematch our socks would be what she calls a "bonding activity."

I'm glad I'm not in Justin's bunk. One night, someone sealed the toilet with plastic wrap. You can imagine what happened the first time one of the boys tried to pee!

I am learning to swim, which is pretty important when you are at camp. For one thing, unless you can swim eight laps . . . . . I can't yet, but I bet I will soon . . . . . you can't go out to the climbing raft, which is the coolest place at camp. I am definitely going to get there before the summer is over.

But the most important news is that I have found an activity that I love more than anything I've ever tried . . . . horseback riding! I wish you could meet Cinnamon. That is the name of the horse I ride, and I love her.

I love you too.
You are the best aunt ever.

Your favorite niece,

Amber

Chapter Twelve

The curtain is about to go up on Cushetunk's first talent show of the summer.

I, Amber Brown, do not have a talent. At least, not one I want to display onstage right now. I've been spending all my free time learning how to take care of Cinnamon, and I don't think knowing how to shovel horse poop counts as a talent. If it did, I would be a star. According to Carrie, horses make about fifty pounds of poop a day.

Holy poop! Good thing it doesn't all come out at once!

Justin is going to perform tonight. But he wouldn't tell me what he is going to do. He said he wants it to be a surprise. "I am sure you're going to like it," he promised.

So I am ready to be the best audience ever. At least I think I am ready. Then the first act comes on. It is Hannah Burton doing her floor routine from gymnastics. She has glitter in her hair. I wonder if she saved it from my birthday celebration. She gets big applause when she does a backward double flip. I have to admit she is good. I applaud with everybody else.

Hannah puts her hand on her heart and smiles at us as if she was just crowned Miss Cushetunk.

I want to puke.

Most of the next acts are from the older kids. One guy plays guitar and sings a song he wrote himself. A tall girl juggles five balls. Two brothers do a tap dance.

I am just thinking that I would like to learn to tap-dance when Carrie comes onstage. Before she can say anything, Cleo runs up to her, shouting, "It's all around me . . . . . it's all around me!" She sounds terrified.

"What?" Carrie cries. "What's all around you? WHAT'S ALL AROUND YOU?!?"

Cleo points to her stomach and shouts, "My belt!"

Carrie and Cleo crack up. So do we in the audience.

They take a bow.

Then Carrie says, "For our final act, Justin Daniels and Treasure Jackson have a song for you."

Is this the surprise, that he's doing a duet with Treasure? When did this happen?

Justin and Treasure stand side by side. Looking very serious, they start to sing. I recognize the tune immediately . . . . . it is the Camp Cushetunk song. Only they have written new words for it.

Cushetunk, our pet skunk,
You should not let your gas out!
Quick, the Glade!
He just sprayed!
I am likely to pass out.
Quick, hold your nose
Or you're apt to die.
The stench grows ever stronger.
Cushetunk, our pet skunk,
We can take it no longer!

At the end of the verse, the two of them start to gag and cough. They stagger around in a circle, then collapse on the floor, twitching and pretending to choke.

Everyone is laughing and clapping. I am sooooo proud of Justin. I should be proud of Treasure, too, I guess. Not only

was the song the funniest thing ever, their voices sounded really good together. They must have practiced a lot. When did they do that . . . . and how come I didn't know about it? And why does thinking about it make me feel so strange?

I go backstage to tell Justin how great he was, but there is already a crowd around him and Treasure. When I finally I get to him, I say, "Justin, that was hilarious!"

His smile is so big you can see every bit of his braces.

I smile back. "Why didn't you tell me

you could sing? I mean, I knew you could sing . . . . . we do it in the car all the time. But I didn't know you could sing like that! And in public!"

Justin shrugs. "When we moved to Alabama, Mom made me join the junior choir at our new church. She said it would be a good way to get to know people. It turned out that I love it. I even joined the chorus in school and had a part in our musical this spring."

I am surprised and a little annoyed. Why didn't I know about something that was so important to Justin? "You need to write to me more often," I tell him.

Justin makes a face. "I'm not so good at that. Sorry."

"So how did you and Treasure end up singing together?" I ask.

He shrugs again. "We just started goofing around on the climbing raft and came up with that song. The other kids out there thought it was so funny they talked us into doing it for the talent show."

I'm happy for Justin, but a little upset too. Not just about Treasure, but that I still can't swim well enough to be a raft kid. I wonder what else I am missing because I can't go out there.

Then Hannah makes it worse. "We laughed our heads off when Justin and Treasure made up that song," she says. "Too bad you weren't there, Amber."

Talk about skunks.

After the crowd breaks up, we head back to our bunk. When I climb onto my bed, I find an envelope on my pillow. Written on it is *To Amber, From Her Secret Admirer.*

I have never imagined having a secret admirer. Could it be from Justin? Part of me wants it to be . . . . part of me thinks that would be too weird.

When I open the envelope, there is a

sudden whirring that makes me jump. "Whaaaa!" I scream.

I think it's a giant bug.

It falls off my bed onto the floor.

Cleo shouts too.

Grace gets to it first. She's got a shoe ready to squash it. Then she starts laughing. "This is made from a bent paper clip and rubber bands," she says. "Where did it come from?"

"It was in this envelope," I tell her. "It was booby-trapped!"

I don't want to show them the envelope because I don't want anyone to see what was written on it. I know they would tease me about thinking I have a secret admirer when all I really have is someone who wanted to play a joke on me. It would be a big laugh.

Then I notice that someone is laughing already.

It is Hannah Burton, of course.

Chapter Thirteen

I, Amber Brown, am about to do the thing I love most at Camp Cushetunk . . . . . be with Cinnamon.

Carrie has asked me to come to the stable after her last morning class. She said she has a special surprise.

Cinnamon is saddled up, waiting for me.

I go over to her. She lifts her head and her ears flick forward.

"She knows you," Justin says.

I didn't realize he was there. He is sitting on the fence. He is not the only one there. Hannah is standing behind him.

"We just finished our riding lesson," Justin says. He takes off his helmet. His hair is sweaty and clings to his forehead.

"Justin and I are in the same riding group," Hannah tells me.

I know their group is just learning to trot. I am already doing figure eights on Cinnamon . . . . . at a canter! This makes me smile a little, but I decide not to say anything. I don't want to end up sounding like Hannah.

Carrie comes out of the stable. "Ah, there you are, Amber. I've got a surprise for you. Kind of a treat for all the extra work you've been doing here at the stable."

"What is it?" I ask eagerly.

She points to a pole lying in the middle of the ring.

"What's that for?" I ask.

"She wants to see if you can walk over it without tripping," Hannah says.

Justin snorts. He sounds a little like a horse.

Carrie turns and shoots Hannah a look. Hannah spreads her arms in a "What did I do?" gesture.

Turning back to me, Carrie says, "I thought we would start working on the basics of jumping today."

I can hardly believe my ears. I turn to Justin. "I've been dying to try this."

Justin grins at me. "I want to stay around and watch."

"Me too," Hannah says. "It could be pretty funny."

I don't want her there, but I don't know how to get rid of her.

The phone in the stable's office rings. Carrie sighs. "I've got to get that. I'll be back as soon as I can. In the meantime, check Cinnamon's tack, Amber."

Justin wrinkles his brow. "What does 'check the tack' mean?"

"She's planning to put the horse on a bulletin board," Hannah replies.

I scowl at her. "The tack is horse talk for saddle and bridle. I'm even learning to tack her myself. That means put her saddle and bridle on and make sure it's all perfect."

Justin looks impressed. Hannah looks bored.

I stroke Cinnamon's neck. Her coat is smooth and velvety. I slip my hand under the cinch, which is the strap that wraps around Cinnamon's belly to hold the saddle in place. It is nice and tight.

I pat Cinnamon again and say, "I have to pee. I'll be right back."

Hannah giggles. "You tell your horse when you're going to pee? I bet she doesn't tell you!"

Hannah has a point. Horses pee whenever they want.

"I gotta go too." Justin jumps down from the fence.

Hannah rolls her eyes. "This feels like third grade. You two couldn't go anywhere without each other."

Justin blushes and looks at the ground. As we walk behind the stable to the Porta-Potties, I say, "I can't believe you're hanging out with Hannah."

Justin shrugs. "It's more like she's hanging around with me. Carrie told me that you were coming, so I stayed after my riding lesson to see you. Hannah decided to stay too."

We go into separate Porta-Potties.

When I go back to the rink, Justin is already there. Hannah is sitting on the fence close to him.

I ignore them and go up to Cinnamon. "We're going to start to jump today," I whisper to her.

I put my left foot in the stirrup and grab the pommel of the saddle. As I swing my right leg up, the saddle starts to slip. I am

sliding under Cinnamon! I fall out of the saddle and land with a thud against wet ground . . . . . which is strange, because it hasn't rained in days.

Justin runs to me. "Amber, are you okay?"

I get to my feet. Cinnamon is looking at me as if she doesn't understand why I am not on top of her, where I belong.

Carrie comes running out of the stable. She looks worried. "Amber, are you all right?"

I nod, embarrassed. "I don't know how I fell off."

I hear giggling. It is Hannah.

"What are you laughing about?" I ask.

"Cinnamon peed at the same time you and Justin did. I was going to warn you. Sorry." She giggles again.

I glare at her. "It's not funny."

"That's enough, Hannah!" Carrie grabs Cinnamon's cinch and says, "Amber, this is way too loose . . . . . I told you to check it."

"I did," I tell her.

"Well, it's loose now," Carrie says. She lifts the flap from Cinnamon's saddle and tightens the cinch. "Are you ready to start again? It's important to get back up on the horse. Both for you and Cinnamon."

What I really want to do is go back to the bunk and change my clothes, but I nod and hike myself back into the saddle. Once I am up, I stroke Cinnamon's neck.

"It's not your fault," I whisper. I look down at Hannah, who is whispering to Justin. I am pretty sure that I do know whose fault it is.

"Focus, Amber," Carrie says as she leads me into the ring.

This makes me feel like I am back in school, since it seemed like all any adult said to me toward the end of fourth grade was "Focus!"

Carrie is still talking. Yikes! I had focused on "focus" and not her.

"I want you looking straight through Cinnamon's ears. It's a bad habit to look down, especially when you jump. You won't actually be jumping now, but even so, you should practice good form. As you get close to the pole, let your hands move forward over Cinnamon's neck. We call that the release."

"Why?" I ask.

"You're releasing her to jump. If you

pull back, you're going to stop her instead. It can feel scary to let the reins go loose at that point, but if you don't, she'll balk and shy."

This is making me nervous. I'm glad we're starting by just having Cinnamon trot over a pole that's on the ground!

"You have to use your legs and your balance. The reason you're such a natural rider is that you've got great balance."

This is a surprise to me. No one has ever complimented me on my balance before.

"Go into a trot," Carrie orders.

I nudge Cinnamon with my heels and cluck to her. Instantly she responds. I start to post. That's using my legs to go up and down with Cinnamon's movements.

As we approach the pole, I learn forward for the release, just like Carrie told me.

We go over the pole in one smooth motion.

"Beautiful," Carrie calls.

I hear clapping. I look over. It is Justin.

"You did great, Amber," Carrie says.

I take Cinnamon around the ring and over the pole several more times. The wet spots on my pants from Cinnamon's pee are starting to bother me, so even though

I am having a good time, I am a little relieved when Carrie says, "All right, that's enough for today. You need to clean up and get ready for swimming. Bring Cinnamon to me. I'll take care of her."

I slip down from the saddle and hand the reins to Carrie.

Now that I'm not focused on riding, my jeans feel disgusting. They smell too.

Carrie lowers her voice and says, "Next time I tell you to check the cinch, make sure you do it."

I bite my lip. I don't want to tell her again that I did check the cinch.

I glance at the side of the ring. Hannah is whispering to Justin.

I walk over to them. Hannah glares at me as if I'm interrupting something.

"You looked like you really know what you're doing," Justin tells me, jumping down from the rail. "See you . . . I gotta go get changed for swimming."

"Amber and I do too," Hannah says. "See you at the raft."

Groan. I have to walk back to our bunk with Hannah.

"Justin is so much cuter than I remember," she says to me. "It's too bad you took that tumble in front of him . . . and too bad you landed in pee."

She giggles but she won't look at me. That's when I know . . . . I just know . . . . Hannah Burton was the one who made me fall in Cinnamon's pee.

Chapter Fourteen

"You can't be certain Hannah did it," Kelly says.

"Sure sounds to me like it was Hannah," Brandi replies.

It is afternoon free time, and we are sitting under Herbert. That is what we named the big tree halfway between our bunks where we like to meet to talk. I have just told them what happened at the stable this morning.

"It wasn't just the saddle," I say. "Hannah has been pranking me since we got here. First it was the hair gel on my pillow."

"Then there was that 'secret admirer' envelope," Brandi says.

Kelly makes a face. "Yeah, that was mean!"

"And then today the saddle," I say. "Falling in Cinnamon's pee was the worst! It's time for revenge. I need a prank that will make Hannah's hair stand on end."

Brandi sits up straight. "Bulletin! Bulletin! Bulletin! Hannah Burton is scared of the Cushie Monster!"

"That's right!" Kelly says. "Remember how nervous she got while we were talking about Cushie when we were out on the party boat?"

"What are you suggesting?" I ask.

Brandi smiles. "What if we make Hannah think that the Cushie Monster has decided she should be its next victim?"

My eyes get wide. "I love it! Only how do we do it?"

Kelly scrunches up her face for a

minute. Then she rubs her hands together. Using a voice like the witch in the *Wizard of Oz* movie, she says, "These things must be done delicately."

"What's that supposed to mean?" Brandi asks.

"Well, we can't just go up to Hannah and tell her that we were talking to Cushie and found out that she's out to get her. We've got to build up to it somehow."

"Oh! Oh!" I cry. "You know the Marshalls, the family my dad rents his apartment from? Well, one time, Dylan wanted to scare his little sister Savannah."

"I remember that," Brandi says. "You told me your father is afraid Dylan is going to grow up to be a criminal mastermind."

"What did Dylan do?" Kelly demands. "And why don't I know about it?"

"You were away at your grandmother's," I tell her.

"So what did he do?"

"Well, he worked out a four-step plan. He says things have to happen in fours."

"I thought they happen in threes," Kelly says.

"According to Dylan, it's three and what he calls a 'topper' . . . that's the biggest thing of all. And you always go from the smallest to the biggest. So first he told Savannah this spooky story about a monster that lives under beds."

"All kids think there is a monster under their beds," Kelly says.

"Right, so that was easy," I say. "But he added details. He told her that the monster liked crackers and bananas and little girls, in that order. So the next night, he made a trail of cracker crumbs leading under her bed. Savannah is kind of a slob, so when she told her father about them, he just thought it was a mess she had made herself. Dylan waited a few days, then left a banana peel on her pillow. That was the third thing."

"Wow, that was nasty," Kelly says. "I'm glad he's not my brother. So what was the topper?"

"He waited a few more days, then he snuck into the room and hid under her bed. He was planning to make scary noises and kind of thump the mattress. He figured she would get so scared she would go running for her father and then he would get out and go to his own room and play innocent. That was where he made his big mistake.

"Savannah was too scared to get off the bed, so she just kept calling for her dad. When he came in and she said there was something under the bed, he told her not to be silly. But she kept insisting, so he said he would look to be sure. It turned out Savannah was telling the truth . . .

there was something under the bed . . . . . Dylan. He was totally busted!"

"Wow. That was some plan," Kelly says. "Except we don't want to get busted."

"Right," I say. "So we'll have to be careful. And with three of us, it will work even better."

We start brainstorming about what we can do to convince Hannah that Cushie is after her.

"What if we have Cushie send Hannah a letter?" Brandi suggests.

"No one's going to believe that," Kelly tells her.

Brandi scowls. "Don't you remember what Mrs. Holt taught us? The first rule of brainstorming is you never shoot down an idea when it is suggested."

"Right," I say. "Just get the ideas out there."

Kelly blushes a little. "Sorry. You're right."

"Okay," Brandi says. "Now, the first thing is to convince Hannah that Cushie is on the move . . . . . up from the lake and into the camp."

"How about a stinky pool of water?" Kelly suggests.

"Brilliant!" Brandi cries. "How do we do it?"

"Oooh! Oooh! I know how to get a stinky pool of water," I say. "Manure tea!"

"That's disgusting!" Kelly says.

"Of course it's disgusting," I say. "That's the point."

"No, I mean it's disgusting that you thought of it."

"I didn't think of it—it's a real thing! Carrie told me about it. Gardeners use horse or cow poop and water to make an organic fertilizer."

"Okay," Brandi says, "but you have to make it!"

I shrug. "No problem."

I am so used to shoveling horse poop by now that the idea doesn't bother me.

"But how do we make Hannah think that she's the one Cushie is after?" Kelly asks.

We stand up and pace. I don't know what good this is supposed to do, but I saw it in a movie once, and it seems like a good idea. We walk around Herbert several times.

"I've got it!" Brandi cries. Then her shoulders slump. "Never mind. I don't got it."

We start walking again.

Kelly stops. "What if . . . oh, never mind."

We change directions and walk the other way around Herbert.

"Snow White!" I cry.

"Huh?" Brandi asks.

I smile. "Who does Hannah think is the prettiest girl in the camp?"

"That's easy," Kelly answers. "Herself."

I nod. "Right. She's like the queen in *Snow White* going, 'Mirror, mirror, on the wall, who's the fairest of them all?'"

Brandi wrinkles her nose. "I still don't get it."

"I do!" Kelly says. "We tell Hannah that Cushie always goes for the prettiest girl in camp."

Brandi nods. "Perfect! So what's the next thing? We need something to convince Hannah that Cushie really is coming after her, slimy tentacles and all."

"Slime!" I cry. "We can use hair gel, just like Hannah used on me."

Brandi shakes her head. "She would figure out what it is pretty quick."

"Oh! I know where to get some good slime," Kelly says. "Remember when we made modeling dough in crafts class last week and that one kid put in too much water?"

Brandi nods. "Right. He got total slime instead! A smear of that on a window would look just like a tentacle mark!"

"This is great," I say. "But what do we do for a topper?"

Brandi rubs her hands together. "Hehhh-hehhhh Hannahhhh!" she moans in a gurgly voice. "Hannah, I neeeeeed you."

"I don't get it," I say.

"In the radio lab I can make a recording that we can play outside Hannah's window. We can do all kinds of things to a voice, make it really weird and spooky. That will definitely scare her."

I love this plan.

I love my friends.

I love that I am finally going to turn the tables on Hannah Burton.

Chapter Fifteen

I, Amber Brown, am shoveling poop into a bucket.

In secret.

This is not something I ever thought I would be doing.

Manure tea seemed like a better idea when I thought of it yesterday than it does now that I am actually making it. I sure hope this is going to be worth it.

I use a hose to fill the bucket, then carry it into an empty stall. I put it in a back corner, where I don't think it will be noticed. It will need a day or so before it is ready.

On Day Two of Operation Cushie, Kelly, Brandi, and I go to check on the brew.

"It's perfect," Kelly says. Her voice sounds funny because she is pinching her nose shut.

"Perfectly disgusting," Brandi says. "Which is exactly what we want! Operation Cushie: Stage One commences tonight at nineteen thirty hours."

"What the heck is nineteen thirty hours?" I ask.

Brandi sighs. "That's seven thirty."

Kelly scowls at her. "Well, why didn't you just say that?"

Brandi smiles. "I think we should use military time for Operation Cushie. They use a twenty-four-hour clock. I learned about it from my uncle, the one who's in the navy."

I review the plan in my mind. First, we're going to make a "Cushie footprint."

This will be a shallow hole scooped out at the edge of the path to our bunk area. It's where I will pour the manure tea when the time is right. We can't do it in advance because it won't take long for the water to sink into the ground.

After supper, everyone will be going back to their bunks to change because it is "pajamas at the movies" night. Kelly is supposed to keep Hannah talking down at the mess hall so that all the other kids will be ahead of them.

I will be hiding in the trees near the "footprint," and Brandi will be the lookout. When Brandi signals that Kelly and Hannah are coming, I'll pour the "tea" into the "footprint," then scoot back to hide in the bushes.

The rest will be up to Kelly.

I, Amber Brown, hate mosquitoes. Mosquitoes, however, seem to love manure tea. I think I am surrounded by every mosquito in camp.

I remind myself that sometimes you have to suffer for art. And I want Operation Cushie to be a work of art, one of the greatest pranks ever pulled, gold medal for our age group.

I hear Brandi whistling the camp song. That's my signal. I step out of the bushes and pour the tea into the "footprint." I slip back into the bushes. A moment later, Brandi is beside me. "They're almost here!" she whispers. She sounds really excited.

We peek through the leaves.

Kelly and Hannah are chatting away. Suddenly Kelly stops. *"Eeeuuuw,"* she says. "Do you smell that?"

Hannah stops and sniffs. Then she sniffs again.

I think it is funny that when people think they smell something bad, they sniff twice to make sure.

"Oh, yuck," she says. "What is that?"

"Who knows," Kelly says. "Let's get going. I don't want to be late for the movie."

They walk a few more steps, then Kelly stops. "Look!" she cries, sounding scared.

I did not know she was such a good actress.

They both stop at the edge of the stinking puddle.

"Footprint," Kelly whispers.

"What?" Hannah asks.

"Footprint!" Kelly hisses. "Cushie footprint."

"Yeah, right," Hannah says.

"All I know is that everyone in our bunk says Cushie is on the move. She's coming up from the lake and snooping around near the cabins. If you see a pool of stinking water, that's one of her footprints. Don't get any on you! That's supposed to attract her."

Hannah walks carefully around the pool of yucky water.

Brandi gives me a thumbs-up.

Stage One of Operation Cushie is complete!

• • •

I, Amber Brown, am wide-awake. Usually I am one of the last in our bunk to get up, but this morning I am awake even before the bugle sounds. That is because I am so eager to see if Stage Two of Operation Cushie is in motion.

The reason I don't know for sure is that it was up to Brandi and Kelly. Were they able to sneak out of their cabin last night and put the slime on the window by Hannah's bunk?

Finally I hear the bugle. I stretch and pretend to yawn. Then I climb down from my bunk and head for the bathroom. I pass Hannah's bunk. YES! The slime is there!

"Yikes!" I cry, pointing. "What's that?"

Treasure and Hannah sit up. "What's what?" Hannah snarls.

I just point. Hannah turns toward the window.

Treasure jumps down from the top bunk. "Whoa, girl," she says. "That is nasty."

It really is nasty . . . . . a long streak of green slime smeared across Hannah's window.

All the girls gather around Hannah's bunk to stare at the slime.

"I heard a rumor that Cushie is on the prowl," Grace whispers.

Carrie comes out from her room. "What's going on?"

We all point at the window.

Carrie bends so that she can see it. She rolls her eyes, then goes outside. We watch her through the window as she examines the green streak.

"Well?" Hannah says when Carrie comes back in.

She scowls. "It must have been one of the boys. Typical middle-of-the-summer stupid boys' trick."

Hannah doesn't look convinced.

Brandi stands next to Hannah in the breakfast line. I stand three people behind them so I can listen.

"Is it true?" Brandi asks Hannah.

"Is what true?"

"Everyone is saying that the lake monster slimed your window."

"I don't want to talk about it!"

"Well, it would make sense if she did," Brandi continues. "I'm doing a news story on Cushie, so I've been talking to some of the older kids. One of them told me that she always goes for the prettiest girl in camp."

Kelly comes up to them. "I heard about the slime on your window," she says to Hannah. "That must have been scary."

"She doesn't want to talk about it," Brandi says.

"Did you tell her about who it goes after?" Kelly asks.

We are so, so bad.

It is afternoon free period. Kelly and I are standing under Herbert, waiting for Brandi. I am starting to get worried. "What if she couldn't do it?" I say.

"Stop fussing," Kelly says. "Look, there she is."

Brandi comes running up, a big smile on her face. "Who rocks?" she demands.

"It depends," Kelly says. "Do you have it?"

"Oh, yeah!" Brandi says.

"You rock!" Kelly and I say together.

What Brandi has is the recording that will give us our topper.

"Can we hear it?" I ask.

She looks around, then says, "Gather close. We don't want anyone else to hear. I'll set the volume real low."

We make a circle, and Brandi turns on the recording.

Out comes the weirdest voice I have ever heard . . . . . . low and burbly . . . . . . almost as if it's coming from underwater. Even though it's broad daylight and I know it's just a recording, it gives me a chill.

"Holy mackerel!" Kelly says. "Is that you?"

Brandi shakes her head. "I got Orion, our counselor from the camp radio station, to do it."

"What did you tell him?" I ask.

"Nothing," Brandi says. "He likes goofing around with sound and electronics, so he just thought it was fun to do." She hands me a small plastic thing. "Okay, this is the remote. You push here to start. I'll slip over to your bunk tonight before lights-out and put the recording I made on the ledge outside Hannah's window. Wait until after lights-out. Then, whenever you want . . . push the button!"

I put the remote in the pocket of my shorts.

I am so happy!

"Lights-out," Carrie calls.

We scramble into our bunks. I have no

intention of going to sleep, of course. I need to stay awake so I can play the recording.

Then Carrie surprises me by saying, "I need to have a short meeting with Maria about the next talent show."

Maria is the counselor for Brandi and Kelly's bunk.

"We'll be on the path halfway between the two cabins if you need me. But I want it quiet, understand?"

I told myself that I would wait at least half an hour after lights-out before pushing the button, but now I think it would be better to do this while Carrie is out of the bunk. I wonder how long she will be gone. I wish she had told us, then I realize it wouldn't make any difference because I don't have a way to tell time. Now I wish I hadn't left my pig-taking-a-bubble-bath alarm clock at home.

I decide to wait ten minutes.

I start counting in my head. "One Mississippi. Two Mississippi." Then I stop and try to figure out how many Mississippis it will take to get to ten minutes. Six hundred! That's too many. And why did Mississippi get to be the timekeeping river anyway? I bet the Amazon is jealous. Just because it's missing one syllable?

The bunk is really quiet. No one is even whispering.

Finally I can't stand it anymore.

I push the button.

The voice that comes through the window is not as loud as I expected, but somehow that makes it even scarier.

"Haaannnnaahhhhh! Hannnaaahhhh! I waaaaaannt yoouuuuuu. I neeeeeeeeed youuuuuuu."

I thought that would be it, but it starts again, this time even louder.

"HAAANNNNNAAHHHHH!

HANNNAAAHHHH! I WAAAAANT
YOOUUUUUU. I NEEEEEEEED
YOOUUUUUUU."

Hannah shrieks and bolts for the door.
I figure she's going to get Carrie, but a
few seconds later, I hear her scream.

Suddenly the lights go on. I see that Grace has hit the switch.

"What's happening?" Cleo cries. "Where did that voice come from?" She sounds terrified, which makes me feel guilty.

The other girls are out of their bunks. I join them. They all want to know where the spooky voice came from. I know, but I don't know what's happened to Hannah, and I'm kind of scared about it.

"We have to go see if Hannah needs help," Grace says. "Grab your flashlights!"

"I don't think we should go out there," Cleo says.

"We have to!" Treasure declares.

But as we start out the door, we hear Carrie shout, "Back inside, all of you! Get in your bunks. I'll be there in a few minutes."

We wait. It seems like a long time. I expect Carrie to come back into the bunk with Hannah any second. I know she'll yell at us like she did when Hannah put hair gel on my pillow, but that would be better than this waiting.

Carrie finally comes back. She looks serious. Hannah isn't with her. I get a bad feeling in my stomach.

Everyone starts to call out questions again.

"Quiet, everyone!" Carrie yells.

The bunk falls silent.

"All right, everybody . . . . . I want you to stay in your beds. I have to take Hannah to the infirmary. I'll have a counselor come in here to take over in a minute. In the meantime, nobody move. Is that clear?"

Her voice is fierce.

We all nod.

"Is Hannah all right?" I ask.

"I said no talking!"

I shiver in my bed.

As soon as Carrie leaves, everyone does talk, of course. Everyone but me.

A few minutes later, a counselor comes in, and everyone asks about Hannah.

"I don't know anything," she says. "But it's after lights-out and Carrie asked me to make sure you stay quiet."

I lie in my bunk, staring at the ceiling. I still have one more thing to do, but I can't do it until everyone is asleep. I do not worry about falling asleep myself . . . . . I am too upset for that.

I wait until the room is completely silent . . . . . . then I wait some more. The counselor has gone into Carrie's room. I know she is asleep because I can hear her snoring. Normally I would think that was funny, but right now nothing is funny.

When I finally think it is safe, I slip out of my bunk. If anyone wakes up, I will say I am just getting up to pee.

No one does.

I open the door as quietly as possible and slip out of the cabin. Then I go to

Hannah's window and get Brandi's recording. I don't want to do this, but I owe it to Brandi. I don't want her to get blamed for this mess.

When I am back in my bunk, I still cannot sleep. I can only think one thing. *I am not a bad kid, but I've done a bad thing. I am not a bad kid, but I've done a bad thing. I am not a bad kid, but I've done a bad thing.*

I think it all night long.

Chapter Sixteen

As the sun rises, my spirits sink.

Hannah's bunk is still empty.

I am terrified. What if something really bad happened to her?

I have never been so scared.

Miss Flo comes into our bunk and I am even more scared.

Miss Flo claps her hands and orders, "Girls! Circle! Now!" Quickly we form up around her.

Miss Flo looks at us. "My first announcement is that Hannah is going to be okay."

Everyone cheers, including me.

Miss Flo holds up her hands and we get quiet. "However, she does have a badly sprained ankle and will have to stay off it for a while. We have called her parents, and Hannah has asked to stay at camp. I am proud of her.

"I am not proud of what happened here last night. I am not saying that someone from your bunk is responsible for the prank that scared Hannah, but I do want to assure you that we will find out who did it. If any of you have information you think we should know, come to Carrie or me. All right, that's it for now. Make your beds and get dressed for breakfast."

I am relieved. I am terrified. I did not know it was possible to feel both things at once.

Everyone is whispering. I keep wondering if they know it was me.

Can you go to jail for a prank?

As we head for the mess hall, I realize that Brandi and Kelly won't know what happened. Fortunately we have already planned to meet at Herbert right after breakfast. I am not looking forward to it.

They were just helping me. What if we all get kicked out of camp for what we have done? It will be my fault.

"Amber, are you all right?" Carrie asks. I did not realize that she was walking next to me.

"Sure," I say. "I'm just thinking."

She gives me a funny look but walks on.

Breakfast is awful . . . . . . and I'm not talking about the food. Cleo is sitting at a table with Kelly. As Cleo whispers to her, Kelly's eyes widen. She twirls around and stares at me, looking panicked.

"At the tree," I mouth.

She nods. Then she goes over to Brandi and whispers to her.

Justin comes over to where I'm sitting. "I just heard about Hannah. Is she okay?"

I can't answer him. I think I am going to cry.

"Wow, I never thought you would get so choked up about something happening to Hannah," he says.

That only makes things worse.

The first thing Brandi says to me when we get to Herbert is "Did you get my recording?"

She looks terrified.

"Right here." I hand it to her.

She heaves a sigh of relief.

"So what happened, anyway?" Kelly asks. "I mean, I know Hannah got hurt, but I want to know the whole story."

When I am done telling them, Kelly says, "I don't think they'll know it was us."

"Why not?" Brandi asks.

"Remember Amber said Carrie thinks the slime was a stupid boy trick? If we're lucky, they'll think the whole thing was a prank cooked up by some of the boys. But since it wasn't, they won't be able to prove it. That way no one gets in trouble."

"So we'll be in the clear." Brandi sounds relieved.

I nod. But somehow I don't feel relieved. "I never wanted Hannah to get hurt."

"None of us did," Brandi says. "But it's not really our fault that she tripped."

I'm not sure that is true.

As the day goes on, I start to relax a little. I still feel terrible about what happened to Hannah, but the idea that we might not get caught is better than a milk shake on a hot summer day.

Like a milk shake, it doesn't last long. Especially because it actually is a hot day, and Hannah shows up at the lake during swimming. Her ankle has an ACE bandage on it and she is using crutches.

Soon there is a small crowd around her. Hannah loves being the center of attention, so it's almost like I've done her a favor. At least I try to tell myself that, but the idea is so dumb it embarrasses me.

I feel like I should go over and tell her how sorry I am that she got hurt. But I worry that if I try, I will blush and give myself away.

I tell myself Hannah wouldn't want sympathy from me anyway, since she has never liked me. But then Cleo comes up from behind and grabs my arm. "Hannah is here!" she exclaims. "Let's go see her."

When we reach the group surrounding Hannah, Cleo says, "It's so brave of you to come to the lake after you were so afraid of the Cushie Monster."

Hannah looks up at her. "The Cushie Monster isn't real!" she snaps. "I know that. I wasn't afraid. I was just going to get Carrie."

I know that's a big fat lie, but I can't say it out loud.

"I was just the victim of a stupid prank," Hannah continues. "Carrie told me that whoever did it is going to get in big trouble."

She unwinds the bandage. "The nurse told me that swimming is good for my ankle," she says. Then, sounding tragic, she adds, "It's about the only thing I can do."

Treasure and Grace help her hobble into the lake.

"Isn't she brave," Cleo murmurs.

"Brave," I agree, since I can't think of anything else to say.

"I'm gonna go swim too," Cleo says. "See ya later."

I think I had better get over to where Pete is waiting to give me my Polliwog lesson. But before I can take a step, Brandi is beside me. Her eyes are wide and she is pale.

"What's wrong?" I ask, frightened by the look on her face.

She glances around to make sure that no one is near us, then says, "Amber, there's no way I'm not going to get in trouble for this! I just realized that Orion will have to tell Miss Flo that he made that recording for me."

It takes me a minute to remember that Orion is the counselor Brandi works with at the camp radio station.

"I'm so scared," Brandi says. "What if Miss Flo sends me home?" She takes a deep breath. "But don't worry. I'm no snitch. I won't tell that you and Kelly were involved."

She tries to smile at me. I know she thinks that what she said will make me feel better.

It doesn't.

What it does do . . . . . . is tell me what I have to do.

Chapter
Seventeen

I am standing at the door to Miss Flo's office. The door is closed. It is not too late to turn back . . . . . I can still change my mind.

Actually, I can't. This is my mess and I have to fix it.

I lift my hand to knock on the door. I almost hope she won't be in. Except that would be bad, because I don't think I would have the courage to come back again.

I knock.

"Come in!" Miss Flo calls.

I take a deep breath. I so want to turn and run. Instead, I open the door.

Miss Flo is not alone. Orion is in the room too.

"Amber," Miss Flo says. "Can you make it quick? I don't have much time."

I know why she doesn't have much time. Orion has told her about Brandi and the recording. And since Brandi and I aren't in the same bunk, Miss Flo doesn't think I had anything to do with what happened.

"It was my idea!" I blurt out. "Brandi only made the recording because I asked her to and because she is my friend. I didn't mean for anyone to get hurt, honest! I just got sick of Hannah picking on me and pranking me!"

That's as far as I get before I start to blubber.

Orion stands up and leads me to a chair.

I see that Miss Flo is writing something on a notepad.

"I'm not a bad kid," I sob. "I didn't know this would happen!"

Tears and snot are streaming down my face.

Miss Flo shoves a box of tissues at me. "Wipe up, stop crying, and start at the beginning."

I do, but I manage to leave Kelly out of it.

When I have finished, Miss Flo turns to Orion. "Will you please bring Brandi Colwin to the office?"

"It wasn't her fault!" I repeat. "The whole thing was my idea. Are you going to have us arrested?"

"No, you are not going to jail," Miss Flo says.

"Are we going to have to leave camp?"

"Amber, I would like you to be quiet now."

Somehow that is scarier than anything Miss Flo has said so far.

I shut my mouth, wondering what happens to kids like us. Miss Flo said we weren't going to jail. But what about reform school? I don't want to have to leave my old school and all my friends.

I wonder if there will be an article in the newspaper. My parents will be so embarrassed to have such a bad daughter.

I would never have guessed that being in trouble with the camp director would be even scarier than being sent to the principal's office.

Finally, Orion comes back, but not just with Brandi. He has Kelly with him too. My friends both look really frightened.

Kelly looks at me and says, "I told him if Brandi and you were in trouble, I should be too. We did it together."

I turn to Miss Flo. "I was the one who wanted to get back at Hannah. They were just helping me. Honest, Miss Flo, whatever you want to do to us should just be me, not Brandi and Kelly."

Miss Flo sighs. "Amber, for the last time, be quiet!"

I start to cry again, but at least this time I do it quietly, with just a few tears running down my cheeks.

Miss Flo makes Brandi and Kelly give their versions of what happened.

When they are done, Miss Flo folds her hands on her desk.

Then she tells us our punishment.

Chapter
Eighteen

When I finally leave Miss Flo's office, I can't stand to go to any of the afternoon activities.

I don't want to be with my friends.

I don't want to talk to anyone.

There is only one place I do want to be, one place that feels safe . . . . . the stable. Horses don't gossip. Horses don't ask you questions. Horses don't giggle and point.

Sometimes I wish I was a horse. It would probably make me a better person.

I get the currycomb and hoof pick out of the bucket and go to Cinnamon. She nuzzles me. She lets me lift her leg, and I clean the dirt out from around her horseshoe.

The horseshoe my father gave me is dangling from my neck. I don't want to think about him now . . . . . or my mom.

I am brushing Cinnamon when Justin walks into the stall. He leans against the wall and watches me for a minute. Finally he says, "You okay, Amber?"

I shrug.

He shakes his head. "Man, you really did it this time, didn't you?"

I nod.

"So is it true that Miss Flo made you and Kelly and Brandi call your parents and tell them what you did?"

I nod again.

"Come on, talk!" Justin says. "You don't have any reason to be mad at me."

I put down the brush. "I'm not mad at you," I say. "I'm just embarrassed because

I did something that caused so much trouble."

"Yeah, but you survived the Cushetunk Monster," he says. "I mean the real one . . . Miss Flo!"

That actually makes me smile.

"So is it true that you had to call your parents and tell them what you did?" he asks again.

I nod again.

Justin sighs. "That bad, huh?"

I can't hold it in. "Justin, it was awful."

"So they were really mad?"

"They were mad, but that wasn't the worst part. I had to make the call in front of Miss Flo so she could make sure I really told them what I had done."

"I don't see what was so bad about that. Miss Flo already knew what you had done."

I can feel tears starting. "You don't understand. Miss Flo set up a conference call, so I had to tell both my parents at the same time. We were on speakerphone . . . . . which meant Miss Flo got to hear my parents blaming each other for what I did. Mom said Dad always loved playing pranks, even when they hurt people's feelings, and I must have got it from him. Dad said Mom was so wrapped up in Max she hadn't been disciplining me properly. Then he yelled at Miss Flo for having me and Hannah in the same bunk. Then my mom told him to calm down, and they ended up shouting at each other over the phone. It was horrible."

Justin's eyes widen. "My mom used to tell my dad about some of the fights your folks had," he says. "I overheard her a couple of times when she thought I was sleeping. I never wanted to tell you about it, but I guess they had some real humdingers."

It feels really weird that Justin knew

more about my parents' fights than I did. I was already ashamed of myself. Now I am ashamed of my parents, and somehow that is even worse.

I start to really cry.

Then Justin does something that surprises me. He puts his arms around me.

He is not being romantic. He is not being boyfriend-y. He is just being my always and forever best friend.

I put my head on his chest and cry until I can't cry any more.

Chapter Nineteen

I never thought I would say this, but I, Amber Brown, do not want to talk anymore.

Unfortunately I don't have a choice. Carrie has called a bunk meeting. "Right after dinner," she tells us. "Everyone must be there . . . . . no exceptions!"

Hannah is on her bunk with her foot propped up on a pillow. She is glaring at me.

She and I haven't spoken. I know I am going to have to apologize to her, but the idea makes me sick to my stomach . . . . . not because I don't owe her an apology, but because she should also be apologizing to me.

"All right, kids," Carrie says. "Circle up!"

I sit as far away from Hannah as I can.

Carrie begins. "Miss Flo wants us, as a bunk, to get to the bottom of these troubles. I told you on our first day I wanted you to have each other's backs. That hasn't really happened . . . . . you haven't taken care of each other. As you all know by now, last night Amber played a prank on Hannah that ended up in her getting hurt."

"It wasn't just last night. What about the green slime on my window?" Hannah snaps.

"That was part of the same prank," I say.

I immediately wish I hadn't.

Carrie turns to me. "While I admire

168

how creative and carefully planned your prank was, Amber, I think it would be a good idea to use your energy in more positive ways. The point of this meeting is to work out a way for the people in this bunk to live together peacefully and cooperatively for the rest of the summer."

"It's not all of us," Grace protests. "The trouble is between Hannah and Amber."

"I didn't do anything!" Hannah says loudly. "And even though I'm the one that got hurt, Miss Flo called me into her office and told me she wanted no more of my picking on Amber. I told her I didn't even know what she was talking about."

This really makes me angry. "Hannah has always hated me. She's been pranking me from the beginning!"

Hannah actually looks puzzled. "What are you talking about?"

"The hair gel on my pillowcase, to begin with."

"Um, actually, that was me," Treasure says.

I blink. "Why?" I ask, feeling hurt. "I never did anything to you."

Treasure shrugs. "I was planning to prank everyone sooner or later. I just started with you because your name begins with A. But Carrie got so cranky about it, I decided to stop for a while. Sorry. I didn't mean for you to take it personally."

I feel a little embarrassed that I got this wrong.

"Hannah has it in for me," I insist. "What about that booby-trapped letter? She figured it would be hilarious to make me think I had a secret admirer and then have it turn out to be a joke."

"But you do have a secret admirer," Cleo says.

I can hardly believe what I am hearing. "What do you mean?"

She blushes a little. "That letter came

from Colin. He asked me to put it on your pillow. I didn't tell you before, because he begged me to keep it secret. He really does like you, Amber. Justin told him that you love jokes. He found out how to make that whizzer in a book and thought you would think it was funny. It was supposed to be a present. He was just embarrassed to let you know it was him."

"Boys are such dips," Grace says.

"Goofnagles," Shannon agrees.

"Dorks," Cleo adds.

"Mutton-headed ding-dongs," Treasure suggests.

Hannah wraps her arms around her chest. "So," she says defiantly. "Everyone agrees . . . . . I have done absolutely noth-ing to Amber."

Cleo raises her hand.

Carrie nods to her.

"Actually, you're mean to Amber a lot," Cleo says softly. "You say terrible things to her, and you're always trying to put her down."

I am so grateful to Cleo for standing up for me.

Hannah looks amazed at this. "Well, I still never pranked her."

"Oh, yes, you did," I say. "The worst thing of all was when you loosened the cinch on Cinnamon's saddle and I fell in the pee!"

I turn to Carrie. "You were there, remember? It was the day you were starting to teach me to jump. You went to answer the phone and Justin and I left Hannah alone with Cinnamon while we went to the restrooms. When I came back, Hannah laughed her head off when I fell into Cinnamon's pee."

"I didn't do anything!" Hannah shouts.

"Don't lie!" I say. "You laughed."

"Okay, I laughed. It was funny. But I didn't do anything to your stupid horse."

"She probably didn't," Treasure says. "Hannah's pretty much afraid of horses."

"Shut up!" Hannah snaps.

"None of that, Hannah!" Carrie says sternly. Then she turns to me. "Amber, did you check the cinch?"

"Yes, right before I went to the bathroom."

"How about when you came back? Horses love to fool you. They blow up their bellies and then the saddle can get loose. That's why we check the cinch just before mounting."

Carrie says all this very gently, but I feel like I've been punched in the gut.

"You made a lot of assumptions, Amber," Carrie says. "Acting on assumptions is a good way to get into trouble."

"See?" Hannah says. "I am totally innocent."

"Not totally," Carrie tells her. "How many times have I had to ask you not to

put Amber down? Your words are very mean sometimes."

"You're not kidding," Shannon says. "I know how I would feel if somebody talked to me the way Hannah talks to Amber."

Hannah blinks as if she can't believe what she is hearing.

Cleo raises her hand again. But this time she doesn't wait for Carrie to nod to her. "It's awful being in the bunk when those two hate each other so much," she says. "Sometimes it gives me a stomachache. I really want our bunk to be a friendly place."

"Me too," Grace says.

"Me three!" Shannon adds.

"Make it four," Treasure says. "I didn't come to camp for this kind of garbage."

I look at Hannah. It's hard to imagine us being friends, but it would be nice if we could at least stop being enemies.

"Hannah," I say. "I am sorry I did the prank that got you hurt."

"Well, you should be." She turns to Carrie. "I don't think it's fair of you to make this about me. It's really all Amber's fault."

"Gaaaaah!" Treasure screams. "Don't you have ears, girl? Haven't you heard a thing we've been saying?"

Hannah shrinks back as if Treasure had slapped her. "So what do you want from me?"

"Something that will stop this sniping," Shannon answers.

"Okay," Hannah says. "How's this for a solution? How about Amber and I don't talk to each other for the rest of the summer? That could work."

"If that's what she wants, I could do that," I say.

Carrie shakes her head. "That's not a solution. Silence can be cruel too. Not talking and holding on to grudges doesn't solve a thing. It can be like a slow poison."

She looks sad for a moment, as if she is remembering something bad. Then she gives herself a shake and says, "Let me tell you a poem. I learned this from the woman who was teaching me English. It's by a man named Edwin Markham. I keep a copy with me all the time.

"He drew a circle that shut me out—
    Heretic, rebel, a thing to flout.
But Love and I had the wit to win:
We drew a circle that took him in!"

Carrie looks around the group. "Bigger circles, my dears. Bigger circles." She stretches, then adds, "All right, it's been a long day . . . . . . and a tough one."

"You're not kidding," Grace mutters.

"But we didn't fix it yet," Cleo says.

Carrie shakes her head. "You can't fix a problem this big in one meeting, Cleo. All I wanted to do was make a start. I think we've gone about as far as we can go for now. It's time to get some rest."

Everyone is quiet as we get ready for bed. But it's not a mean silence. It's a thoughtful one.

After I wash up, I climb into my bunk.

The lights go out, but it's a long time before I get to sleep.

Chapter Twenty

Dear Mom and Dad,

I am sending this same letter to both of you, even though it means I have to copy it over. (So you know I must be serious.)

First, I have to say that I am really sorry I got in trouble here and had to call you about it. The good news is, I think I have learned something from what happened. More about that later.

Second . . . . . oh, this is hard to write, but I have to say it. You really embarrassed me with the way that you acted on the phone. You were trying to blame each other for the way I behaved. Maybe it's not each other but both of you.

The reason I got in trouble is that I couldn't find a way to make peace with Hannah . . . . . just like you haven't been able to find a way to make peace with each other.

We had a bunk meeting last night, and Carrie from Kiev talked to us about how staying angry is never good for you. She said that not talking and holding grudges can do a lot of damage.

It made me so sorry that Hannah and I hate each other . . . . I'm going to try to do something about that.

At the end of the meeting, Carrie taught us a poem that I really love. I wanted to send it to you, because I love both of you so much. Here it is:

He drew a circle that shut me out—
Heretic, rebel, a thing to flout.
But Love and I had the wit to win:
We drew a circle that took him in!

Today, I am going to try to draw a
circle big enough to hold both me and
Hannah. I am going to offer to help her
get around while she is still on crutches.
I am a little afraid that she will laugh at
me for this, or say something mean, but
I won't know until I try.

Can you try not to be so mad at each
other anymore?

I Love You,

amber

Chapter
Twenty-one

"You have got to be kidding!"

That is Kelly. We are standing at Herbert, and I have just told Kelly and Brandi that I was wrong about Hannah being the one behind all the pranks.

"You mean we got in all that trouble for nothing?" Brandi exclaims. "Bulletin! Bulletin! Bulletin! Amber Brown is on my poopyhead list!"

"I know, I know!" I say. "I'm sorry!"

"Even so, it was a pretty awesome prank." Kelly is smiling.

"True that," Brandi agrees.

The three of us look at one another and grin. Silence may not always be good, but I know that we are all thinking the same two things. One . . . . . despite how it worked out, we had fun putting the prank together. And two . . . . we will never say that out loud.

"But you're still on my poopyhead list," Brandi says.

"So what do you want me to do?" I say. "Drink manure tea?"

Brandi and Kelly both make gagging noises.

Hannah and I have made it through lunch without talking to each other. But it's not an "I hate you" kind of silence. It's more of a "What am I going to do about you?" kind of silence.

You would think silence is silence, but this really does feel different.

As we leave the mess hall, I see her

struggling with her swim bag and her crutches.

I walk over. "Hannah, can I carry that for you?"

She bites her lip and hands the bag to me without saying anything.

We walk down the path to the lake. We move slowly, of course, because of Hannah's crutches.

Neither of us talks.

This is awkward, but at least it's a start.

I am not terribly good at not talking. Finally the silence gets to me. "Hannah, I didn't realize until last night that I was wrong and you really hadn't done any of the pranks. It's my fault you got hurt, so I think it's kind of fair to help you carry your stuff around . . . . . . but only if you don't mind."

She looks as if she's about to say, "You'd be the last person on Earth I'd want to touch my stuff." But that is just me making another assumption. All she says is "Okay."

Well, at least it's a word.

At the waterfront, Hannah goes over

to her swimming group and I go to join Colin and Pete at Polliwog Pond.

I watch Colin swim two laps doing the crawl. He lifts his head and waves at me. I think about telling him I know about the "secret admirer" letter.

I decide it would only embarrass him . . . and me too.

Instead, I call, "Colin! That's the farthest you've gone yet!"

Pete grins. "My two favorite Polliwogs are close to passing that lap test."

Pete has us both swim laps. I try doing the crawl, but it makes me really tired.

At the end of the second lap, I look up and see Hannah standing on the dock. "The sidestroke is better for distance," she says. "If you do that, I think you can make eight laps with no problem."

Then she swings her crutches around and heads back to the beach.

When swim period is over, I carry her swim bag to the bunk. Neither of us says anything as we walk, but it feels different somehow.

Cleo smiles when she sees us come in.

"I'm heading up to the stables," I tell Hannah. "Do you need anything before I go?"

"What are you going for?" she asks. "It's not your riding period."

"I love to brush Cinnamon and just hang out with her. Do you want to come? There's a chair in her stall you can rest on."

"Well, I am bored," she says. "Normally during my free period I practice gymnastics. But I can't do that because of my ankle."

I know she is trying to make me feel guilty. Or, at least, I assume that . . . . Maybe she just doesn't know how bad that makes me feel. I want to shout at her to stop poking me . . . . I already said I was sorry. Instead, I count to ten. Max has told me that this is a good thing to do when you want to keep your tongue from getting ahead of your brain.

"Come on." I pick up her backpack.

Hannah sighs, but she gets up on her crutches.

At the stables I open the door to Cinnamon's stall. Hannah hangs back.

I hook Cinnamon's halter to the stable wall.

"You can sit over there." I motion to the chair in the corner.

Hannah doesn't go. She seems to both want to stand near Cinnamon and get away.

"She's big," Hannah says.

"Let her smell you," I suggest.

"That's what Carrie said, but horses have big teeth."

"Just let her smell the back of your hand," I say. "You can keep your fingers away from her."

Hannah holds out her hand. Cinnamon bows her head a little.

"I like her blaze," Hannah says.

I see Carrie looking at us over the stall door. She nods to me, then walks on without saying anything. Even without words I feel she is pleased with me.

"Well, that was something I never thought I would see."

It is after dinner, and Justin and I are walking to the craft shack.

"What do you mean?" I ask.

"You and Hannah Burton walking side by side without flames bursting out of your heads."

I laugh. "I doubt we'll ever be friends. But it's nice not to feel like we are enemies."

Chapter Twenty-two

Carrie blows her whistle. "All right, you guys, I want this place spotless before your parents get here!"

It is visitors' weekend. Most parents will be coming up the first day. But the camp has added a second day for kids like me whose parents are divorced.

I guess my parents aren't the only ones who can't get along.

"You've only got an hour," Carrie warns. "The parental floodgates open at ten!"

I can't wait to see Dad. I want to show

him Cinnamon. And I've got another surprise for him as well.

We get busy cleaning. I figured I would help Hannah, but everyone pitches in. And she does as much as she can, which is nice.

Our bunk has never looked so clean. I didn't realize that "visiting day" would mean "cleaning morning."

In Dad's last letter he told me that he is so excited to see me that he wishes the camp would let parents in even earlier than 10:00 A.M.

This "earlier than 10:00 A.M." thing is not like Dad. He is more likely to be late than early. In fact, Mom and Dad used to fight because sometimes he was late picking me up.

We wait for our parents at the flagpole. The camp has set up some tables with coffee and snacks. There are games to play, but since you can see the parking lot from the flagpole, most kids are busy watching out for their parents.

Suddenly I see a flash of red. It's the Hot Tamale. I start running down the hill to the parking lot. Then I stop. Another car has pulled in next to the Hot Tamale . . . . Max's car! Did Mom and Max get mixed up and forget that today was Dad's day to visit?

I have a sick feeling in my stomach. I DO NOT want Mom and Dad to get in a fight right here in the parking lot!

Dad and Miss Isobel get out of the Hot Tamale. Mom and Max get out of their car. All four of them are waving and smiling.

What the heck is going on?

I stand still. I don't know who to run to or what to do. Mom and Dad talk for a moment, then start toward me.

Max and Miss Isobel hang back.

"Amber!" Mom cries when she is closer.

She is smiling and holding her arms out.

I look from her to Dad.

"What's going on?" I ask.

"We need to talk to you," Dad says.

"Is there someplace we can go?" Mom asks. "Just the three of us?"

"What about Max and Miss Isobel?"

"They're fine," Dad says. "They know we want to talk to you."

"Ummmm . . . . . do you mind sitting on the ground?" I ask.

Mom and Dad look at each other and shrug.

"The ground is fine," Mom says. "It's summer and we're at camp!"

"Then I know a great tree for sitting under. Its name is Herbert. It's where Brandi and Kelly and I go to talk."

"Let's go," Dad says.

"Just a second," I say. "I haven't hugged Max or Miss Isobel."

I run to them and give each a quick hug.

Then I lead Mom and Dad to Herbert.

Part of me is scared . . . . . part of me is confused . . . . . part of me feels like I don't even know what my parts are. What is going on here?

One thing that's going on is that we are walking together. I can't remember how long it's been since the three of us did that.

"So this is Herbert?" Dad asks when we get there. He puts his hand on the trunk. "Pleased to meet you, Herbert."

I giggle.

We all sit.

"A mighty fine tree," Mom says.

"Clearly a good place for planning nefarious pranks," Dad says.

"Now, Phil," Mom says. But she doesn't sound angry. It's almost playful.

"Sorry," Dad says.

"Will you two tell me what is going on?" I cry. "My head is about to explode!"

They look at each other. Then Mom reaches into her purse. At the same time, Dad reaches into his pocket. They each pull out a piece of paper.

"This is what's going on," Dad says.

I realize they are both holding my letter.

"Are you mad at me for what I wrote?"

Mom shakes her head and I can see that there are tears in her eyes. "Oh, honey. We're not mad at you. We're angry at ourselves because it took our wonderful daughter to make us look at how we've been behaving."

"It wasn't a pretty thing to think about," Dad says. "I know you were embarrassed by how we acted on the phone with Miss Flo. I'm embarrassed too. And ashamed. After I got your letter, I decided I needed to talk to your mom."

"And I decided I needed to talk to your dad," Mom says. She smiles. "It was a nice moment. Your dad called just as I was picking up the phone to call him. Tell her what the first thing you said was, Phil."

Dad smiles. "I said to your mom, 'We gotta make a bigger circle.'"

He stands up and puts out his hands. Mom stands up too. "Come here, Amber," she says softly.

I stand up.

They put their arms around me.

"We can't live together," Dad says softly. "But we can sure as heck do a better job at getting along for your sake, Amber."

I start to cry.

But not because I'm sad.

Chapter
Twenty-three

I, Amber Brown, have been told many times that I have a vivid imagination. But I would never, ever, ever have dreamed I would be introducing Cinnamon to Mom, Dad, Max, and Miss Isobel all at the same time.

When I call her name, Cinnamon sticks her head out of the stall.

"Oh, she is most beautiful," Miss Isobel coos.

"You get on top of that big thing?" Max asks.

"I always loved horses when I was a girl," Mom tells me.

"Let's see you ride, Amber," Dad says.

Carrie, who has been watching this, has me show them how I've learned to put on the saddle and bridle. I check the cinch. Twice. Carrie winks at me.

I swing my leg over the saddle. "Walk on," I say to Cinnamon as I take her into the ring.

Carrie sets up a low jump in the center of the ring, then nods to me. I nudge Cinnamon with my knees and she moves into a trot. We circle the ring a couple of times, then go cleanly over the jump.

Carrie gives me a thumbs-up.

"That's wonderful, Amber!" Mom cries.

I get down from the saddle.

"I have one more thing to show you," I tell the four of them. "Just let me change into my swimsuit."

When I am ready, we walk to the lake. Justin's parents are there, standing on the dock. Mom and Dad must have warned them that they were going to show up together, because the Danielses do not fall into the water.

I turn to Mom and Dad. "Remember how I told you I couldn't swim? Well, watch this!"

I run to the end of the dock and jump in.

Using the sidestroke, I swim out to the raft. Justin is there, along with a whole lot of other kids. It is Justin who comes to the ladder and holds out a hand to help me scramble up.

He smiles. "Welcome aboard, Amber. I knew you would get here sooner or later."

The climbing part of the raft slopes above us. Together we make our way to the top.

Standing side by side, we look back to the beach. Our families are there, Justin's two parents and my mixed-up double family.

But we can see more, much more.

The beautiful blue lake surrounds us like a giant circle.

Beyond it are the woods . . . . and the world.

I, Amber Brown, am one happy camper.